Original Edition – *Uncommon Partnership* -

I0537902

GEN

SAN FRANCISCO

Occy Yang with Katie Gorick

GEN SAN FRANCISCO

Copyright © 2015 by Occy Yang

Printed in the United States of America
ISBN: 978-0-9966935-3-0

Learn more information at:
www.gensanfran.com

ACKNOWLEDGMENTS

I wish to thank Katie Gorick, the other co-writer, for persisting through the whole process of creating this book for the last two years. Jenny Liu also has provided wonderful artworks.

This short book is dedicated to our beloved entrepreneurial generation of America that keeps our society interesting and inspiring. We also do not forget the passionate "you" who anonymously have grown a humble startup project somewhere in the world.

.

Chapter 31

Matthew's phone rang at precisely 9:00 AM, and he knew without looking that it would be Scarlet. He'd been up since 7, drinking coffee and fidgeting while he watched the news and waited for her call.

"Good morning, Scarlet!"

"Good morning yourself. Ready to talk shop?"

"Yes ma'am!"

"Good. I should warn you I don't really know where to begin. I've never started a company before."

"That makes two of us."

"But I figured getting our vision straight would be a good place to begin. Let's hammer out some of the details of exactly what it is we're going for here."

"Great, I agree. So the basic idea is to start a small fashion boutique. With designs inspired by the work of Adelina Bianchi, and possibly some influence from organic food images. Making use of 3D printing technology to create unprecedented new designs and structures… How's that?"

"It's a start. I think we should also focus on making our materials and production process very environmentally friendly. If we're going to do this whole thing with the 3D printing, we should also be forward-thinking in regards to our waste and carbon footprint."

"That's an excellent idea. We could brand ourselves as this very futuristic and trend-setting company, using cutting-edge technology and preserving a better world for posterity."

"Right. I don't know of any other fashion lines out there right now doing anything like this. I think with my background in materials science we'll have an advantage over any possible competition."

"I agree. So I guess our target demographic would be upper-middle class, at least until we can find a way to drive costs down without compromising our principles. We'll design for both men and women. Most likely the younger crowd, who tend to be more open to new technologies and more passionate about saving the planet."

"That all makes sense to me. I think our biggest issue is going to be funding. This 3D printing technology is not cheap. At all. And of course we'll need to find a space to operate out of. How are we going to finance it all?"

"I was thinking of creating a Kickstarter account, at least to begin with. We can both work our connections through friends, family, coworkers, to find anyone who might be looking to invest. I have a chunk of money in savings that I can contribute, as well."

"Okay. While you get the Kickstarter up and running, I'll look into pricing for a 3D printer, as well as what it might cost to rent out one at a university or private facility, at least for the first few prototypes. I'll also do some research on environmentally friendly textiles."

"Perfect. I'll start putting out feelers to find some potential investors, and continue working on design sketches."

"Sounds like a plan. Check back in tomorrow with progress?"

"Works for me. Talk to you tomorrow, Scarlet."

"Bye, partner."

Matthew hung up the phone and hopped up from his armchair, nearly spilling his coffee. He dashed to his desk and began to work on the Kickstarter account. He discovered that nearly 2,000 fashion projects had already been successfully funded with the site's help, a total of over 40 million dollars. He couldn't help but feel a flurry of hope at seeing the numbers.

His hope began to falter, though, as he discovered the statistics for project success. Only 18% of projects seeking less than 50,000 dollars reached their funding goals, and only 7% of projects seeking 100,000 dollars or more. Matthew decided their best shot would be to start with a (relatively) smaller fundraising goal, and plan on using a university 3D printer or purchasing a small-scale one to use to furnish their product prototypes. Hopefully, these prototypes would inspire enough interest that larger donations would come in to fuel full-scale production.

He set the target funding to 50,000 dollars, with a time limit of six months. The timing would be tight, but neither he nor Scarlet could afford to commit to the project much longer than that without any kind of paycheck. If they hadn't reached their goal in six months, they would set down their sketchbooks and return to the real world.

For a project description, he did his best to summarize what he and Scarlet had discussed that morning; a forward-thinking fashion startup based on the principles of sustainable, environmentally-friendly production and a fresh take on the vintage styles of Adelina Bianchi, making use of cutting-edge 3D-printing technology to manufacture materials.

Matthew had just hit the "Complete" button to finalize the Kickstarter project when his cell phone rang for the second time that morning. It was his mother.

"Mom?"

"Matthew! I called your office but they said you were working from home today. Are you feeling okay?"

"I'm fine, Mom. I just wanted to be able to make some phone calls in private and it can get noisy around the office."

"Oh, okay. You haven't had any more problems with your head, right?"

"None at all. I'm perfectly healthy. So what's up Mom? Why are you calling?"

"Do I need to have a reason?"

"Well no, I guess not."

"But as it happens, I do have a reason this time."

"Busted."

"Guess who called me this morning?"

"I have no idea, who?"

"You're supposed to guess, silly!"

"Santa Claus."

"No. Aggie Wright! John's mother! Our neighbors from back in Orange County!"

Matthew laughed kindly at his mother's enthusiasm. She and Mrs. Wright had been tight friends throughout his childhood.

"I remember, Mom."

"She said that she was talking to John and he mentioned you'd stopped by for a visit! She said he was just so happy to see you and catch up like old times."

"I'm glad! I had a great time with him too. I actually spent a night at his apartment in Sacramento."

"What brought on that sudden visit?"

"I was visiting the old house on a whim and I ran into John visiting Mrs. Wright. He invited me to a party up at CalTech so I stayed with him and his roommate afterwards."

"And how is John? He was always such a sweet boy."

"He's doing great, Mom. He's in grad school now. Seems to have a great group of friends there with him."

"I'm so glad to hear it. So how has work been going?"

Matthew hesitated for a moment. He hadn't thought he would have to tell his parents about the company so soon, but having found a partner had given him a new confidence in the plan.

"Well, one of the reasons I'm home today is to work on my start-up?"

"Since when do you have a startup?"

"As of about ten seconds before you called me, actually."

Naturally, Seraphina Kim had endless questions. Matthew fielded them all patiently, starting from his long-repressed desire to express a more creative side of himself, to his decision to express this through fashion design (not including the time travel experience), to meeting Scarlet at the CalTech party and forming a partnership. When he was finished, there was a long silence as his mother struggled to process the new information.

"So… this is not just since you hit your head, right?"

Matthew laughed.

"No, it's not. Well, not exactly. These are feelings I've had for years. But I can't deny that my stay in the hospital helped spark some urgency. A friendly reminder from the universe that there's no time like the present to take a chance and follow your dreams."

"Well then I support you, Matthew."

"Thanks, Mom. I really appreciate it. I'm guessing Dad won't be quite as sympathetic."

Seraphina sighed. They both knew Mark's ferociously practical nature would rebel against his son's sudden desire to leave a steady income.

"Do you want me to tell him?"

"That's all right. I'll tell him myself. Is he around?"

"No, he's at the office."

"All right, I'll give him a call. Wish me luck."

"Good luck Matthew. I love you."

"Love you too, Mom."

Matthew hung up the phone and braced himself for what was sure to be an unpleasant conversation with Mark Kim. He wondered if he would ever outgrow his childlike desperation for his father's approval. Probably not. Either way, this little chat wouldn't do him any favors. With a quiet groan, he punched in the numbers to his father's cell phone. Mark picked up on the second ring.

"Hello, Matthew."

"Hi, Dad. Is this a bad time?"

"No, not at all. I actually just wrapped up the paperwork for the Farnsworth case."

"Oh, good. Look, I wanted to talk to you about something."

"What is it, son? Are you in trouble?"

"No, no, nothing like that. I've… been thinking about making a career change."

"Moving to another company?"

"Well, in a way, I guess. I actually want to start my own company."

"Matthew, you know as well as I do that the market is saturated with consulting firms right now. That's simply not a practical decision right now–"

"No, not a consulting firm. I'm going in a different direction."

"And what direction is that?"

"I… I'm going to start a fashion company. Like… to design clothes."

Mark Kim was silent for so long that Matthew thought they'd been disconnected.

"Dad? You still there?"

No response. Finally, after minutes without a word being exchanged, Matthew's father spoke.

"Why?"

"Why what?"

"Why do you want to design clothes? You have a good job, Matthew. You are lucky to be where you are."

"I know, Dad. But I hate my job. I've wanted to do something more creative for a long time now. And I've realized I'm not getting any younger, so I might as well take a chance and go for it."

"So take a pottery class! You are risking your financial stability, your way of life! For some crazy whim!"

"It's not a whim, though. I've put a lot of thought into this. I'm sure that this is what I want to do. I realize it seems foolish and maybe it is, but I don't care. I don't want to spend my life wondering 'what if'."

"Since when do you know anything about clothes, anyway?"

"Well, I wouldn't claim to be an expert, but I'm learning quickly. I've done a lot of study on the work of Adelina Bianchi – she was a designer in the early 20th century

– and I've got some ideas about some new production techniques, along with my partner."

"Your partner?"

"Yeah. I figured I would need some help to pull this off. So I'm teaming up with a woman named Scarlet Love. She's a materials scientist from CalTech."

"Did you go to school with her or something? Or just post a listing for 'Crazy Assistant Wanted' on Craigslist?"

Ignoring the jab, Matthew blazed on.

"I met her while I was visiting John Wright at CalTech."

"And then what? You wowed her with your extensive knowledge of fashion design?"

"I explained my plans, my motivations, and my vision. And she decided to take a chance on me."

"So she's as big a fool as you."

Matthew didn't respond right away. He'd grown tired of his father's bullying. Enough was enough.

"Well, that's all then, I guess."

Mark sighed deeply. Then came the words that so rarely passed his lips.

"I'm sorry, Matthew."

"You're what?"

"I'm sorry. I've been too harsh. If this is truly what you want to do, and you have a plan in place… then I will find a way to support you. I've spent too many years pushing you to follow my footsteps, and I don't want to lose you. You're too important to me."

"I… wow… umm… thanks, Dad. That means a lot."

"Please, tell me more about your plan. I will try to be more open-minded this time."

And so Matthew started again from the beginning, and told his father about his plan in detail, including his intent to make use of 3D-printing with Scarlet's help, and to market their line as a forward-thinking, environmentally friendly company. By the end, his father's disdain seemed to have subsided. In fact, he seemed *impressed* by the discussion of the innovative textile production techniques, his business-savvy mind perhaps imagining an untapped new market.

Matthew summed up his story by describing the Kickstarter account he had created earlier that morning. Mark had heard of the website, and was pleased to know that his son was using it to seek funding.

"Albert's brother was able to get his film project funded with Kickstarter! I've heard it can be quite effective."

"Hopefully it will be!"

"Look, Matthew… I want to support you."

"I appreciate that, Dad. I really do. It means a lot to me."

"No, I mean financially. I want to show you that I truly support you, even if it's not exactly what I might choose myself. I want to make a contribution to your fund."

"Oh, Dad, you don't have to do that!"

"I want to. Your mother and I have been saving for years, and for what? We don't like traveling, we have plenty to retire on, and we don't have any more children's educations to pay for. We've wanted to start investing for a long time, but we just never got around to it. What could be a better investment than our son's company?"

"Wow, I… I don't know what to say. Are you sure you want to do that? I promise you won't hurt my feelings, I never expected you to get involved."

"I'm positive. You can pay us back when you're a famous designer, huh? I'll take care of it when I get home this evening."

"I… Thank you! Thank you so much. This means so much."

"You're welcome, son. I'm just sorry this wasn't my first response to hearing about your new plan. Anyway, I should get back to work. I'll talk to you later, Matthew."

"Bye, Dad."

Matthew hung up the phone, unable to believe what had just happened. Over the course of one conversation, his father's attitude on the start-up had gone from derisive and condescending to outright supportive. It barely seemed possible.

That evening, Matthew checked on the Kickstarter account. There was one pledge, from Mr. Mark Kim, for ten thousand dollars. Matthew collapsed back into the couch, closed his eyes, and smiled. This was the best he'd felt in a long time.

Chapter 32

"Ten grand? We've got ten grand pledged already??"

Scarlet was beside herself with excitement at hearing the news of Matthew's father's Kickstarter donation on the phone the next morning.

"Yeah! My dad decided he wanted to support me in my endeavors no matter how ridiculous, apparently."

"This is great news. Nice work, dude."

"Thanks. But obviously it's just a start. It's going to take a lot more to get things moving. Did you get quotes for the 3D-printers?"

"Yeah, and they're not pretty. An industrial-sized one would be upwards of 30,000. We could probably get a small one for under ten, but it wouldn't be able to keep up if we get picked up by a retailer. I think the best bet is to use the one at CalTech for our prototypes."

"What would that cost us?"

"Well I have access to it through my lab, so we'd just have to pay for whatever materials we used. I cleared it with my supervisor already. It gets so little use that he doesn't think it will be a problem."

"Excellent. That's good to hear."

"I've also got a lead on a guy who specializes in biodegradable textiles. I'm meeting with him next week."

"Perfect! I'll keep looking for investors for the Kickstarter campaign. If we're using the CalTech printer for the time being, we won't need an office space per se just yet. We can operate out of my house for other operations."

"Sounds good. I can catch a flight there this Sunday so we can chat face-to-face and continue to hammer out some details. Also, if you can have some design sketches ready by then, I can work on converting them into a file we can send to the 3D-printer."

"Fantastic! I'll see you then."

Matthew hung up the phone. He was back in the office today, and he had a lot to do to make up for the previous day's outburst of entrepreneurship. Still, he found himself doodling sketches in his notebook between conference calls throughout the day. He couldn't help it. He was fixated in particular on a design for a women's evening dress, a sleek, asymmetrical gown with a single thick strap and a 3-dimensional starburst design on the chest of the strapless side. The skirt was fitted through the hips, just above knee-length on the strapped side and down to the floor on the starburst side. He visualized the dress in a deep blue, with the starburst design in bold crimson, orange, and yellow, like a sun blazing through the empty sky.

As his office phone rang yet again and jolted him from his dazed state, he quickly closed the notebook and returned it to his desk drawer. He shook his head, reminding himself that for the time being, he needed to perform well at this job if he wanted to fund the next. He picked up the phone and got back to work.

Chapter 33

The week flew by for Matthew. Between working long hours at the office to make up for missed time, and slaving over his design sketches whenever he had a quiet moment, he barely remembered to eat and sleep. He was practically buzzing with excitement by the time Sunday rolled around. Scarlet's flight wasn't due to get in until around 10 that morning, but he was up at 7 anyway. Searching for something to occupy his idle hands, he set about preparing an elaborate brunch of French toast, bacon, fruit salad, and yogurt parfaits.

When the taxi arrived and Scarlet walked in and saw the extensive spread of food on the kitchen table, she laughed out loud.

"I hope you don't expect the two of us to finish all of that!"

Matthew smiled sheepishly and pulled two coffee mugs from the cupboard.

"I got a little carried away. You'll have to take home some leftovers."

He led Scarlet on a quick tour of the main floor of the house, relieved that he had decided to finish unpacking the cardboard boxes that had littered the rooms for too many months. The associates then sat down to eat and drink coffee and exchange pleasantries, but the conversation quickly turned to business. Neither could wait to discuss the week's developments. Matthew went first.

"So… have you seen the Kickstarter recently?"

Scarlet grinned while trying to hide a mouthful of French toast. She gulped down the food with a sip of coffee.

"I have indeed. We're over fifteen thousand as of this morning, right?"

"Yes we are! Apparently the men and women of Bradley, Kim, and Weston have been in a generous mood this week. Might have something to do with a certain terrifying partner..."

"I don't care if it's due to the alignment of the planets. It's huge. And it makes us look like we're worth investing in."

"I sure hope so. Because I haven't had much luck in convincing most of the people I've called to contribute."

"Relax, Matthew. This is good news. Things are moving. Have faith that they'll keep moving. Do you have some designs to show me?"

"Yes! They're right here..."

He scurried to the other side of the kitchen, where he'd left his sketchbook on the counter while he battered the bread for the French toast. Returning to the table, he cleared a space among the dishes and opened the notebook to the sketch of the starburst dress. He'd continued to revise the design over the week and was quite proud of his progress. The lines were powerful but feminine, proud yet approachable. He'd added color, as well, a deep sapphire for the body of the gown and fiery scarlet and gold for the starburst. He had in mind a taffeta or some similar material for the dress, with a 3D-printed polymer textile for the decal.

In addition to the starburst dress, Matthew unveiled four other designs. One was an emerald green hat, inspired by one he'd seen Biani wear in New York. It was wide-brimmed and dramatic, designed to be worn at an angle on the head. There was a silver buckle around the center of the hat, simple and elegant. The next was a women's pantsuit. It was a crimson red, had a high cinched waist in the jacket, and the slacks were flared ever so slightly at the ankles. The buttons on front of the jacket and on the sleeves bore intricate golden designs for detail, which were complemented by a whimsical swirling pattern of gold on the back. Third was a pair of dinner gloves. Matthew had never known anyone in the twenty-first century who wore dinner gloves, but he was hopelessly drawn to the romanticism of the idea. The gloves were off-white, and in different shades of blue and purple were raised designs of music notes. The last sketch was the only men's piece. It was a double-breasted dress jacket, cobalt grey with black and white trim. It was simpler, less showy than the other designs, but the clean lines and sharp cuts drew attention anyways.

Scarlet looked at the designs without speaking for a long time. Her face was expressionless except for the occasional raise of an eyebrow. Matthew couldn't tell if she was impressed or skeptical, but he knew enough to keep his mouth shut while she examined his work. He chewed nervously at his cuticles while she flipped calmly through the pages of the sketchbook, analyzing each drawing thoroughly. After several minutes, she finally lifted her gaze to meet his. As usual, her enigmatic eyes revealed nothing. After a moment's staring contest, she broke into a smile.

"Matthew, I love these. They're amazing."

Matthew gave a loud, surprised laugh of relief.

"You think so?"

"Absolutely. They're really, really good. You've seriously never done this before?"

"Nothing of the sort. But like I told you, Biani made an impact on me."

Scarlet nodded understandingly, and Matthew marveled once more at his luck in finding the only other person in California crazy enough to believe his story.

"Well, I think these are a great place to start. I'll talk to some of my computer science friends about the best approach for making files for the 3D-printer based on the sketches. As soon as the files are ready, we can start printing. At least, if we know what materials we're using. I think I mentioned last week that I have a contact in biodegradable materials?"

"Yeah, you did. Any updates on that?"

"I'm meeting with him on Tuesday. Jamison Stewart. He's a third-year PhD student in materials doing his thesis on environmentally-friendly textile production."

"Sounds perfect for us."

"That's what I thought too."

Scarlet's emerald eyes sparkled with the same excitement Matthew could feel churning in his stomach. A sudden urgency washed over him and he couldn't stop himself from acting impulsively.

"What are you doing later tonight?"

Scarlet tilted her head to one side, like a dog who has heard an unfamiliar noise.

"Well I have a video conference with my lab group from two till four this afternoon. My PI is in Oslo visiting some old colleagues and wants regular updates. And then my flight back to Pasadena leaves at eight tonight. But that's about all I have going on today. But don't worry I wasn't planning to just hang out in your house all day, I was going to find a coffee shop somewhere and get some work done and stay out of your hair and –"

"No, no, I'm not worried about that at all! Stay as long as you like, it's no trouble to me!"

"Oh… well, then why…?"

Her voice trailed off as she squinted at him suspiciously. Matthew shifted nervously in his seat, having second thoughts about his impulse.

"I was wondering if maybe you'd like to get dinner? Tonight? With me?"

The squinty green eyes widened with surprise.

"Oh! Dinner! Umm… Yeah, I don't think that would be a problem. Sure, why not."

Matthew felt his stomach turn somersaults. No backing out now.

"Great! There's a really good Italian place not far from the airport if you're interested… It's kind of a hole in the wall, but the food is really fresh and all homemade."

Scarlet smiled the shy grin of a girl asked on a first date.

"That sounds perfect. Maybe 5:30 or 6 so I can catch my flight?"

"I'll make the reservation now!"

"Awesome. In the meantime, though, I am going to get out of your hair. I'll go set up shop somewhere and get some work done, and we'll touch base later this afternoon?"

"It's a deal."

Matthew stood and escorted her to the front door. He managed to maintain a calm, composed attitude until she had disappeared into a cab towards the city center. He then shut the door and collapsed backward into it with a heavy sigh, simultaneously giddy with excitement and frozen with fear. He had a date with a beautiful woman. But what if he had just doomed his fledgling business?

Chapter 34

Phone calls. Endless phone calls. Matthew knew if he let himself be idle for too long, he would lose his nerve and chicken out of his date with Scarlet. So he busied himself calling anyone and everyone he could think of to find investors for the company. He abandoned all self-consciousness and rang up people he'd never met before, men and women suggested to him by those he did know.

Naturally, not everyone took too kindly to being solicited for investments by a complete stranger on a Sunday afternoon. But some of them were surprisingly open to what Matthew had to say. They listened to his vision, asked questions about his inspirations and design styles, and in a few cases, even agreed to contribute. For someone who'd never placed much faith in networking, Matthew found himself incredibly grateful for the friends and acquaintances he'd gathered over the years.

It was an unexpectedly successful Sunday. By 4:00 in the afternoon, after hundreds of calls, Matthew had managed to find investors to bring the Kickstarter total to over $22,000. One such investor, a woman by the name of Jessica Orson, mentioned that she had helped to fund a number of successful fashion start-ups, and she suggested that Matthew and his business partner attend a gala the following month that would be attended by many of the big and up-and-coming faces in the fashion industry. Flattered and caught off-guard, he blurted out that he and Scarlet would be there before even checking his calendar.

As the afternoon moved steadily toward evening, Matthew decided he needed to put down the phone and get ready for dinner. He stood in front of his closet for ten minutes without touching anything. He wanted to look nice. But not too nice. Not trying-too-hard nice. Definitely not pathetically-chasing-after-a-younger-woman nice. He shook his head to try to chase away the negative thoughts. She was 25, only 7 years younger than him. That wasn't such a dramatic difference.

Almost out of habit, he reached to pick up the light blue tie with the black and silver stripes. The tie he'd picked out to impress Jennifer at the Christmas party over a year earlier. For a moment he stood with the tie between his fingers, feeling the soft threads of silk. A slow smile came over his face, and he let the tie fall to the floor. That was the past. It was time to live in the present.

Even before the tie reached the ground, Matthew was grabbing up articles of clothing. He needed no more time to deliberate. There was no point worrying about dressing for someone else. He would dress for himself. If he allowed the opinions of others dictate his choices, he would end up in the same pattern he'd always been in, allowing someone else's wishes for his life to outrank his own.

Black shoes, black pants, a charcoal-grey button down shirt, and a deep red tie. Simple, clean, sharp.

Since there was never a wait at Mama Lucia's, and the airport was only a five-minute drive from the restaurant, Matthew had made the reservation for 6. This decision had the added benefit of limiting the length of any potential awkward silences after the dinner was over. He'd called Scarlet earlier in the afternoon, and knew that she was holed up in a Caffe Trieste a few blocks away.

At 5:30, Matthew grabbed his jacket and left the house. Scarlet was ready and waiting for him outside of the coffee shop, looking relaxed and calm. Matthew tried to channel the same energy as she hopped into the passenger seat, tossing her backpack into the back seat.

"How was the lab meeting?"

"It was good! My PI was definitely geeking out over his buddy's research in Norway. So we basically just listened to him and didn't have to spend much time getting our own progress analyzed."

"Oh, that's good! I bet it's freezing in Norway right now."

"Haha, Professor Findley was wearing three coats during our video chat. And he was indoors!"

They both laughed warmly, and Matthew felt some of the knots in his stomach loosen. This felt alright. This was good.

"So I managed to track down a few more investors today, too."

"Seriously? You're a machine! Where are we now?"

"Twenty-two. Well, a little over twenty-two."

"Twenty-two *thousand* dollars?!"

"Yup."

Scarlet fell quiet, smiling to herself as she looked out the window at the snow which had begun to fall softly on the city. The darkness of evening had settled in heavily now, stretching its tendrils into each twist and turn of the urban streets, but the thin layer of soft white snow helped to brighten the bleak winter landscape.

Matthew parked the car in front of Mama Lucia's a few minutes before their 6:00 reservation. It was snowing a bit harder now, and they both turned up the collars of their coats as they scurried to the door. They were ushered inside by a clean-cut teenage boy with short blonde hair and long, skinny limbs. The sleeves of his white button-down were rolled up, but it was clear from the gap between his black slacks and dress shoes that he had already outgrown his uniform. He wore a small plastic nametag that read "Steve".

The restaurant was warm and inviting, with clean maroon carpeting and rich wood paneling of a deep brown. The lighting was softened by stained-glass fixtures, but was not so dim that one had to squint to read the menu. There were only a few tables occupied, and Steve led the way to a small booth along one wall. He set down two menus, informed them that their server would be there shortly, and returned to his post at the entrance, stumbling once along the way but recovering quickly.

When Matthew looked up from hanging his coat on the hook beside his seat, he discovered that Scarlet was still staring in Steve's direction, a small grin playing across her lips. He glanced over his shoulder to see what the amusement was, but the boy was just standing by the door, waiting for more customers. He turned back towards Scarlet.

"What are you looking at?"

Scarlet's grin spread a bit wider as she broke her gaze and faced Matthew. A touch of red bloomed across her cheeks, a hint of embarrassment.

"I was just watching the kid. He reminds me of my little brother."

"You have a brother! Any other siblings?"

"A little sister, too."

"Tell me about them."

But at that moment, they were interrupted by the arrival their waiter, a young lady who appeared to be college-aged. She had perfectly straight, raven-black hair, and wide-rimmed glasses. She wore bright green studs in her ears and spoke with a quick, confident clip.

"Good evening sir, ma'am. Welcome to Mama Lucia's. My name is Caroline and I'll be your server this evening. Can I get you two started with something to drink?"

Matthew gestured for Scarlet to order first.

"Umm… iced tea, please? Sweetened."

Caroline began scribbling, but Matthew interjected.

"You sure you don't want a *drink* drink? You do have a flight ahead of you. Probably going to be some crying children aboard."

Scarlet smirked, then glanced back up at Caroline.

"The man makes a good point. I'll take a bourbon on the rocks, please. And a glass of water."

Caroline nodded, revising the order, and turned towards Matthew.

"Blue Moon, please. And a glass of water here too."

Caroline dipped quickly out of sight, and Matthew resumed the conversation.

"So, your siblings?"

"Right! Right. Two siblings, both younger. My sister, Jenny, is a junior at Yale right now. She's a finance major, and she coxes for the men's crew team there. She's pretty tiny."

"Sounds pretty successful, too! Are you two close?"

"Yeah, we are. We try to Skype at least every couple weeks or so just to stay up-to-date on each other's lives. She's got a new boyfriend now! He manages for the hockey team or something. I haven't met him but he sounds like a nice kid."

"That's sweet. And how about your brother?"

At that moment Caroline returned with their drinks. With quick, fluid motions, she set out the drinks and glasses of ice, as well as a pitcher of water.

"Are you two ready to order, or do you need a few more minutes?"

They hadn't even cracked open the menus yet. They looked up, flustered, and Caroline nodded and excused herself, promising to return shortly. Scarlet giggled, a surprisingly girlish sound.

"Whoops… We could not have been less ready for her."

"Poor Caroline. She might be in for a rough night with space cadets in her section."

"Should we actually figure out what we want?"

"For her sake, yeah, we probably should."

They opened the leather-bound menus, which were overwhelmingly extensive. After about thirty seconds of silent perusing, Scarlet snapped hers shut. Matthew glanced up, surprised.

"Made your decision already?"

"In a manner of speaking, yes."

"Oh?"

"You're going to pick for me. You're the Italian food expert."

"Well I'd hardly call myself an expert…"

"Oh, enough with the modesty. Any favorites from your time at Carlo's? Keep in mind I may be the least picky eater you've ever met. I'm basically a human trash can."

Matthew chuckled nervously and returned to his menu, frantically wracking his brain for the perfect dish to recommend. Was seafood trying too hard? Should he steer clear of heavier cream sauces? Did she like spicy foods? Scarlet could see his eyes scanning rapidly back and forth across the text, and she snapped him back to reality by reaching across the table and lightly touching his left wrist.

"Hey. Don't stress over it! I told you, I'm not picky. I was just looking for a recommendation."

"Right, right, sorry. Umm… how about the osso buco? Do you like veal?"

"Love it. That sounds great!"

"Okay, awesome. Any interest in splitting the fried calamari as an appetizer?"

"Few things are better in this life than tiny fried squids."

"Great. And I'll go with the chicken marsala. Phewf, glad that decision is made!"

"Most stressful part of your day?"

"Easily."

Right on cue, Caroline reappeared beside the table.

"Do we need any more time over here?"

Matthew smiled sheepishly, adjusting his collar a bit.

"Nope, I think we've made our decisions. Could we get the osso buco, the chicken marsala, and an order of fried calamari to split?"

"Absolutely. Would you like the calamari first, or everything at the same time?"

"Let's have the calamari separately, please."

A quick nod, a rapid flourish of her pen, and the young server whisked away once more. Matthew relaxed back into his seat, and sipped from his beer for the first time. Scarlet hadn't taken a drink yet either, and she followed his example and lifted the bourbon to her lips. Matthew waited for her to place the glass back on the table before he resumed their chat.

"You were about to tell me about your brother?"

"Oh yeah! So I have one brother, younger. He's the baby of the family. His name is Hayden, and he's a senior in high school right now. Seventeen years old, trying to figure out where he'll be going to college next year."

"What's his first choice?"

"Currently, I believe it's Stanford. He wants to follow his big sis out to California!"

"Where's home for you?"

"Pennsylvania, originally. About half an hour outside of Philadelphia. So my parents are hoping he'll end up somewhere on the East Coast so that it's easier to see him during the year. I think they're rooting for UPenn."

"Wow. Pretty good options across the board! Sounds like you guys have quite the power family."

"We're pretty big nerds, yeah. Mom makes fun of us all the time. How 'bout you, any siblings?"

"Nah, I'm an only child. Pretty boring."

"Where are you from?"

"I grew up in New Jersey. My parents are from South Korea, but both came to the states for college and ended up staying."

"Oh cool! So do you ever travel to Korea to visit family and stuff?"

"We went a couple times while I was growing up. We only ever visited my mom's extended family, though. My dad had some kind of falling-out with his parents years ago and now they don't speak. I have no idea what it was about."

"Interesting… and where did you go to school?"

"I did my undergraduate studies at Dartmouth. Then Oxford for grad school."

"So you're no dummy yourself!"

"Ha ha, I suppose not."

"And you've been all over the world!"

"Well, I've seen some of Europe and South Korea. That's about it. Have you done much traveling internationally?"

"My family went to Italy one summer when I was growing up. And I've taken a cruise that stopped in Mexico. But that's about the extent of my experiences."

"But I take it you want to do more travel?"

"Absolutely. I really want to check out South America. And I've heard Singapore is amazing. Ooh, and I definitely need to see Australia."

"Sounds like quite the world tour!"

The calamari arrived, steaming and smelling delicious. Matthew served a few pieces onto Scarlet's plate, then his own. The knots of stress in his stomach had finally loosened up, and he was having a hard time keeping himself from smiling as he watched Scarlet bite into the tasty fried squid. The dinner was progressing better than he'd expected, and he was starting to feel comfortable in his own skin in the presence of this beautiful, intelligent, passionate young woman.

Both young entrepreneurs continued to sip from their drinks, a warm flush coloring their cheeks. The conversation continued to flow comfortably, effortlessly as they finished off the calamari and Caroline brought out their entrees. Everything was cooked perfectly, seasoned perfectly, presented perfectly. At one point Matthew had the strange and overwhelming feeling that the whole evening was just an excellent dream. Under the table, he pinched his leg, hard, causing himself to grimace. Scarlet noticed.

"You okay?"

"I'm great. Everything is really great."

Chapter 35

Shortly before 7:30, Scarlet set down her tiny espresso cup and glanced at her watch. She sighed.

"As much as I hate to end the fun, I think I should probably be getting to the airport."

Matthew nodded, and quickly flagged down Caroline to get the check. With catlike quickness, she vanished around the corner and reappeared with check in hand. She set it down on the table, and Matthew snatched it before Scarlet could protest. He tucked his credit card into the pocket of the leather folder, handing it back to Caroline. Scarlet frowned.

"You didn't have to do that, you know."

"It's my pleasure. I appreciate you coming all this way to meet face-to-face."

"I was happy to! Things really seem to be coming together, don't they?"

"They do."

For a moment they were both quiet, exchanging shy smiles, before Caroline returned with Matthew's card. He snapped back to reality and stood up abruptly.

"Well, we should be heading out, I suppose."

They exited the restaurant, Scarlet again grinning at the lanky frame of Steve the doorman. It had stopped snowing outside, but the two inches of soft fluff made the evening sparkle in the moonlight. Matthew opened the passenger door for Scarlet, and she snorted at the old-fashioned gesture.

"Who says chivalry is dead?"

They didn't speak during the short drive to the airport, but it was a comfortable silence. Matthew pulled up to the passenger drop-off door, and they looked at each other for a moment, still without saying a word. Her green eyes danced with an enigmatic fire, and a lock of her soft chestnut hair had fallen in front of her face.

An overwhelming sensation overtook Matthew. His heart swelled with a mixture of excitement and fear, and without hesitation he reached out one hand to the smooth skin of the back of Scarlet's neck, drew her close, and kissed her. He kept his eyes shut tight, immediately regretting his decision and fearing the worst, but to his surprise she responded positively, after the initial paralysis of shock. She placed her own hands on Matthew's shoulders and for a moment they seemed to melt together. Her lips tasted of espresso and Matthew thought that in that instant he could die and be perfectly happy.

As they withdrew from their unexpected embrace, they both chuckled sheepishly. Scarlet was the first to speak.

"Well, this was fun."

"Definitely."

"I guess I should get on my plane now, though."

"Right. Probably."

"But I'll talk to you tomorrow, I'm sure."

"Yup, you know where to find me."

"Okay. Have a good night, Matthew."

"You too. Travel safe!"

She exited the car and walked into the airport without looking back. Matthew was relieved, since this meant she didn't see the goofy, uncontrollable smile on his face. He hummed happy songs to himself as he drove home, and that night he fell asleep thinking about the curves of her lips when she smiled.

Chapter 36

As the Kickstarter fund continued to grow, the new business began to take shape. Scarlet had made contact with a friend at CalTech, Jamison Stewart, whose research focused on biodegradable textiles. He had developed a number of blends of cotton, silk, and hemp with the qualities the novice designers desired, as well as eco-friendly synthetic composites of polylactic acid and nitrocellulose which would work well with the 3D-printed portions of the designs.

Scarlet had also enlisted the help of her roommate, who was skilled in the use of a sewing machine, to help put together the prototypes of the initial designs. Meanwhile, Matthew had found a small storefront in downtown San Francisco that was available for rent, which he thought would serve their purposes nicely once they were officially up and running. He also continued to fundraise, and finally one cold call resulted in a lucky break.

The newly supportive Mark Kim had provided his son with a few names of contacts he thought might be useful in the budding start-up. One of these was a wealthy investor in the fashion industry, and a past client of Mark's. He owed the elder Kim for the favorable resolution of his estranged father's estate after he passed away suddenly without a written will. The client's name was Benedict Jenson, but Mark had stressed that he exclusively went by Benny, and resented anyone who did not respect his wishes to be called by his nickname.

Matthew called Benny's office, and a secretary picked up after two rings. He asked to speak with Mr. Jenson, stating that he was an associate of Mark Kim, and was connected after a few minutes on hold while the businessman finished his previous call.

"Benny here. Who's this now?"

"Hello Mr. Jenson – er, Benny. My name is Matthew Kim. I'm Mark's son."

"Mark Kim's son? Huh. I didn't even know he had a kid."

No surprise there, Matthew thought to himself. *I'm not exactly his pride and joy.*

"Yup, I'm his only child. But I guess we're not super close."

"I feel ya there. My dad and I wouldn't speak to each other for years at a time when he was alive. But still, any son of Mark Kim is a friend of mine. Your pops really helped me out a few years back."

"He's very talented, for sure."

"Best in the game, if you ask me! Anyway, I'm guessing you aren't calling just to chat about the father you're not super close with?"

"You guess right. I was actually hoping you might be able to help me out with my new start-up."

"Oh? And what kind of start-up are we talking?"

"A small fashion design company, specializing in 3D-printing and biodegradable materials."

"Mark Kim's kid, a fashion designer?! No way."

"It's a recent career change. Anyway, my dad mentioned that you're a pretty successful investor in the fashion industry, and I wanted to see if I could interest you in helping us fund the new company."

"Hmmm... I can probably swing a few bucks for the son of the guy who helped save my fortune. In fact, I'll do you one better."

"How's that, exactly?"

"There's a gala next weekend in Vegas with a ton of big names in the fashion world. On paper, it's a fundraiser for some group that donates clothes to poor African children or something. But really it's just an excuse for a bunch of wealthy designers and investors to get drunk and rub elbows."

It was the same gala Jessica Orson had mentioned offhand when Matthew had called trolling for investments.

He'd completely forgotten about it... and the fact that he'd claimed he and Scarlet would make an appearance.

"Wow... that sounds... extravagant?"

"Now there's an understatement. Anyway, how 'bout I get you on the list for the party? Then you can solicit money in person instead of over the phone!"

Matthew gave a half-hearted, embarrassed chuckle. Benny's laugh, in comparison, was full and genuine.

"Relax, brother, I'm just busting your chops. I actually don't mind the cold-call at all. But you might have more success with people when you can introduce yourself and shake their hands. So, you in?"

"I – yes, yes please! That would be incredible."

"Cool, consider it done. Anything else I can do for ya?"

"Nope, that's about it... Oh, wait, actually, could you also get my business partner on the list?"

"Oh sure, no problem! What's the name?"

"Scarlet Love."

"You'll both be on the list next weekend. This your cell you're calling from?"

"Yes, it is."

"Perfect. I'll text you the address and itinerary. See ya there, son of Mark Kim!"

"See you soon. Thanks, Benny."

"Don't mention it."

As he hung up the phone, Matthew felt his warm smile give way to a wave of icy-cold panic. What had he gotten himself into? A fancy gala with a bunch of fashion A-listers? He would make a fool of himself and of the company, for sure. Not to mention the question of what one was supposed to wear to a party full of the people who made fashion trends for the rest of the world.

His mind racing, he finally thought of the one person he could call who would make him feel better about everything. With one hand he wiped the chilly sweat that had gathered on the back of his neck, and with the other he dialed

Scarlet's number.

Chapter 37

True to form, Scarlet had been able to address the imminent social gathering from a place of logic and calm. She had patiently allowed Matthew to express all of his fears and concerns, then gently offered solutions. At the end of their long conversation, he was feeling much better and she was looking forward to going to a classy gala in Vegas.

Benny was true to his word and donated funds to the Kickstarter. Five grand, along with a note that he would be happy to invest in stock if the new business made it off the ground. He had also sent along the itinerary and location for the gala, and offered to show the newcomers around and introduce them to a few of his contacts, if they were interested. Naturally, they were.

They had five days to prepare. Scarlet procured the prototypes of each of the initial designs, including a few made entirely of all-natural, biodegradable materials, so that they would have something to show potential investors. Matthew wrote, deleted, and re-wrote a concise but comprehensive summary of their business goals and structure, as well as a plan for early as well as advanced stages of production and finances.

Scarlet had suggested that they each wear one of the new designs to the gala, in order to demonstrate the fit and flow of the articles on a real body. She would wear the sapphire gown with the 3D-printed starburst, and he would wear the cobalt grey double-breasted jacket. He would also wear a ruby-colored handkerchief in his lapel to match the bright starburst on Scarlet's chest.

Meanwhile, the Kickstarter account had grown to over 30 thousand dollars. Matthew still felt a hitch in his throat every time he pulled up the webpage. He was terrified that one day it would load and account would be empty. Zero dollars. Say goodbye to your fashion company. But every day the number grew. It didn't vanish. The dream was still alive.

Matthew and Scarlet did their homework in the days preceding the gala. At Matthew's request, Benny had sent them a guest list, so that they could do some background research on the designers and investors they might meet. They memorized names with headshots they found online, as well as a brief summary of their involvement in the fashion industry to date. They also paid particular attention to the most innovative big-shots, who might be the most willing to believe in an unproven pair with unique design ideas.

Finally the big day approached. They each made plans to fly into Las Vegas, where they would meet up with Benny. They would take his hired car to the event, so that they fit in with the other well-to-do designers. Scarlet would bring the prototypes as well as the gown and jacket that they would wear, and Matthew would bring the business plan and budget. Benny had recommended a respectable but modestly-priced hotel near the airport, where they had reserved a single room with two beds. Scarlet had made the reservation, and Matthew was not positive how to interpret it.

Chapter 38

For once, Matthew wasn't dreaming of the beach.

Colors swirled in loosely-defined shapes. They seemed to retreat from alarming close to a more comfortable distance, taking form as they did. The effect was dizzying and downright intoxicating. Sometimes the amorphous color bands seemed to twirl around one another, and the colors would melt together into a new hue altogether. Elsewhere, a shade would seem to explode into waves of its different components. The shapes arranged themselves, broke apart, changed colors, and rearranged. Eventually they formed their final product; a long, brilliant ball gown. It was as if one had repurposed Joseph's Amazing Technicolor Dreamcoat for use in high fashion. The dress incorporated too many colors to count, and yet they blended together so seamlessly that one could not detect a border.

The gown took on a woman's figure, and began to sway gently. Gradually a form materialized to fill the dress, a form having lightly tanned skin with warm peach undertones, and soft waves of rich brown hair. The last features to appear were those of the face, but as they did, there was no mistaking who they belonged to. Finally Scarlet smiled, fully constructed and glorious in her splendor. Her normally confident green eyes betrayed a trace of doubt.

"How do I look?"

THWUNK.

Matthew's plane to Las Vegas touched down with a seemingly careless aggression. He rubbed his eyes and smoothed out his hair while the cabin rumbled as the wing flaps and brakes fought to arrest the momentum of the aircraft. The man to Matthew's left, a heavyset gentleman with thinning blond hair, was snoring quietly, having somehow managed to sleep through the rather turbulent landing.

In fact, the man continued to sleep right through the taxiing process, and it wasn't until the other passengers were already beginning to file off the plane that Matthew had the heart to wake him. He seemed to actively resist entering the conscious world, and Matthew had to tap his shoulder rather hard to elicit a response. The man eventually stopped snoring with a loud snort, lifted his head, and looked around through squinted eyes. He looked at Matthew, at the plane around him, and at the immobile airport visible through the windows. Then he broke into a wide smile.

"Vegas, baby! We're here!"

The large man hopped up and out of his seat, grabbed a small designer suitcase from the overhead bin, and wished Matthew an "excellent stay in the best city on earth", then dashed off the plane. Matthew waited until the plane was almost empty, then stood and retrieved his own bag, and disembarked.

Scarlet's flight had arrived about an hour earlier, and she was waiting for him at the gate with two cups of coffee in hand. She handed him one as he approached, with only a sly smile for greeting, and turned and began walking towards baggage claim. *All business,* Matthew thought, as he scurried to keep up with her.

It was almost 2:00 PM, and the airport was bustling. Baggage claim was packed with excited travelers eager to start their weekend of gambling, drinking, and general poor decision-making. Matthew and Scarlet battled their way through the sea of humanity to Claims 9 and 4, respectively, and retrieved their luggage. After reuniting, they struggled over to the Ground Transportation exit, where they encountered a serious-looking man in a black suit holding a sign reading "KIM & LOVE". His eyes, facing straight ahead, never wavered until Matthew and Scarlet were right in front of him. He then gave them a single careful once-over, and seemed to find them acceptable.

Mathew extended a hand to shake, which the serious man took without hesitation.

"Hi there, I'm Matthew Kim. This here is Scarlet Love. I take it you work for Benny?"

The serious man nodded, and his hard steely eyes relaxed a bit.

"That I do. I'm Greg. I'll be your driver for the weekend."

Taking one of their bags in each hand, Greg led the way outside to a sleek black limousine idling in the pick-up lane. He opened the back door for his guests, then disappeared around the back to place their luggage in the trunk. Scarlet climbed in first, and Matthew hesitated just a moment so that it wouldn't seem like he was looking at her backside. He crouch-walked to the seat beside her, and the pair exchanged impressed looks at the luxurious vehicle. The black leather seats were soft and ridiculously comfortable, there was a well-stocked minibar along one side of the cabin, and the lighting, temperature, and music could all be finely tuned with a series of buttons and knobs on the ceiling.

Greg slipped into the driver's seat, and glanced over his shoulder at his passengers.

"Anywhere you guys want to stop before we head to the hotel?"

Matthew was caught off-guard, and opened his mouth wordlessly before shrugging.

"Nowhere that I had in mind. How about you, Scar?"

"Nope, the hotel should be fine!"

Greg nodded, and rolled up the partition between himself and the passengers to give them some privacy. As the partition closed, Scarlet grinned, her eyes flashing mischievously as she leaned over to retrieve a bottle of champagne from the minibar. Matthew glanced nervously towards the front of the limo, where Greg was focused entirely on navigating the airport traffic.

"I'm not sure we should open that… this is Benny's limo…"

Scarlet laughed warmly. Her smile was honest and free of worry.

"You think too much, Matthew. Live a little!"

Matthew contemplated for the briefest of moments, but he couldn't resist that smile for long.

"Fine. Let's do it."

With a loud *pop*, Scarlet opened the bottle and poured two glasses as the limousine pulled out onto the highway.

Chapter 39

By the time they arrived at the hotel, Matthew was feeling warm and relaxed. Scarlet slipped the half-empty bottle of champagne into her purse as they climbed out of the limo. Greg retrieved their suitcases from the trunk, and gave them his cell phone number so that they could call whenever they needed a ride. He then tipped his hat to them respectfully, and drove off.

Scarlet checked in at the front desk, and they made their way up to their room on the fourth floor. Matthew entered first, setting his bag on the bed nearest the door. He didn't look back at Scarlet but he felt painfully aware of her presence behind him as he waited to see where she would place her things.

Maybe it was all in Matthew's head, but he could have sworn that she hesitated beside the bed he had claimed before continuing on to the second. He was at once relieved and disappointed by the implications of her choice, but did his best not to dwell on the matter. Doing his best to seem casual and relaxed, he made a show of stretching and then checking his watch.

"We've got a few hours to kill before the gala. Is there anything you wanted to see in Vegas?"

Scarlet never even looked up. She was busy unpacking the contents of her carry-on bag, setting up her laptop on the desk in the corner.

"Unfortunately I have to Skype in for our weekly lab meeting in a half hour, so I won't have a chance to do much exploring. I think I'll head down to the Starbucks in the lobby, since the wifi should be pretty good down there."

"Oh okay, cool. Lab meeting. Right."

"But you should go have fun! Take pictures if you see anything ridiculous out there."

Matthew laughed and promised he would. A few minutes later, Scarlet gathered up her laptop and notebook and headed downstairs to the lobby. Matthew sat down on the bed with a deep sigh. He flicked on the television, deciding he would take a few minutes to relax before heading out to explore the city. But apparently the stress of traveling combined with the alcohol had taken more of a toll than he'd realized, and he promptly fell into a deep sleep.

The impromptu nap was dreamless and peaceful. The room was warm, the lights were dim, and the bed was absurdly comfortable. Matthew didn't stir at all until Scarlet returned from her lab meeting about two hours later. The soft scratching of her key card in the door did not disturb him, nor did the rustling of her bag as she fumbled to return the key to her pocket. She failed to notice her partner sleeping while she struggled with the card, and kicked the door shut behind her. It closed with a loud *thunk*, and Matthew returned to the world of the conscious in an instant. He jolted upright and looked towards the source of the sound. His sudden movements caught Scarlet's attention, and she instantly turned bright-red.

"Oh shoot, Matthew I didn't see you there! I didn't mean to wake you up!"

"No, it's fine! I didn't mean to fall asleep…"

"You must've needed it, then! I'm sorry I woke you."

"Really, it's not a problem. I should probably start getting ready for the gala anyway. I need to review my notes again."

"Okay. Well, I brought you some coffee and a muffin from downstairs. I felt weird sitting in the Starbucks without ordering anything so I bought one of these coffee cake muffins and it was pretty much the greatest muffin ever. I had to get you one to get your opinion. And the coffee is just because it's gonna be a long night."

Matthew laughed, and happily took the coffee cup and paper bag. Scarlet set down her bag and scurried off to the bathroom to take a quick shower to get rid of the "airplane smell", and Matthew retrieved his printed notes on the fashion bigwigs they might encounter, reading through them in bed while he sipped at his coffee. He also munched on the muffin, which was perfectly moist and cinnamon-sweet. Perhaps the most delicious thing about it, though, was that she'd thought to buy it for him. He couldn't help but smile to himself, feeling a bit like a child with a bad case of puppy love.

Shaking his head to try to shake off such thoughts, he refocused himself on the notes. As he scanned through list of names and bios, one in particular stood out to him. A woman named Mary Chin. From the look of it, she'd had a hand in consulting or investing in every major fashion company for the last ten years. She also had a proclivity for unique brands, those that approached the design industry in some fundamentally different way. Perhaps she would see promise in a small start-up based on 3D printing and biodegradable materials?

By the time he'd reached the bottom of his cup of coffee, Matthew was feeling reenergized and alert. He wasn't sure if this was due to the effects of the caffeine, or simply the adrenaline as they neared showtime. Hearing the blow dryer power on in the bathroom, he decided this was a good time to get changed, since Scarlet would be preoccupied for at least fifteen minutes.

The black slacks had been tailored just days earlier to ensure that they would be a perfect fit. Matthew had never spent so much money on a single pair of pants in his life, but Scarlet had ensured him that they needed to be at the top of their game if they were to have any success securing investors. The slacks had been painstakingly ironed, with a crease as sharp and intimidating as a shark's fin.

His shoes were polished to a high shine. The black satin tie was neat and clean. The white button-down shirt was simple and understated, but of very high quality. The star of the outfit was, of course, by design, the jacket. The cobalt gray seemed to reflect a steely glint in Matthew's eyes when he caught his own reflection in the mirror, and he was impressed by his own stylish and professional appearance. The double-breasted design was flattering, lending the appearance of more volume in his shoulders while highlighting his narrow waistline. The bronze buttons gave a spark of warmth to the outfit.

Matthew finished off the outfit with the ruby-red handkerchief, which he folded into his jacket pocket so that only a small triangle was visible. He combed his hair, and spritzed himself with cologne. He was adjusting his silver watch when Scarlet emerged from the bathroom. Only this was no Scarlet he had ever seen before.

Matthew actually felt his jaw drop a little bit. The fabric of the starburst dress hugged every curve of her body like nothing he had ever imagined. The material seemed to shimmer faintly when she moved, lending her an intriguing ethereal character. The starburst itself was full of so much color and warmth that it could have been a flame, and the design was intricate but easy to look at. The sharp slit up one leg of the dress revealed Scarlet's smooth, tanned leg, looking fantastically toned in the strappy, sapphire-blue heels. Finally, her long chestnut hair had been curled into gentle waves, which seemed to pay no mind to gravity as they framed her face. It took Matthew nearly a full minute to regain his ability to speak.

"You… I don't… um… wow."

Scarlet laughed.

"Are you always this articulate?"

"You look… incredible. I just… Wow. Damn."

"You're not so bad yourself. Man, the stitching on the jacket came out perfectly, didn't it?"

"It did. But I just can't get over that dress. We actually did a pretty good job with all this."

"Yup. But it won't mean anything if we can't convince these rich folks to give us some of their money. You ready to schmooze?"

"Ready as I'll ever be. Networking was never my strong suit."

"Relax. They'll all be drinking. Should be a willing audience."

"Easy for you to say. You look like *that*."

Scarlet grinned and tossed her hair playfully over one shoulder, dropping her chin and making seductive eyes at Matthew.

"Excuse me sir, but please allow me to tell you about an investment you won't regret."

"I'm sold."

Chapter 40

Climbing into Benny's limousine for the second time that day, Matthew found himself wondering if this was all just one long, complicated dream. Scarlet brought him back to earth with a sharp elbow to his ribcage.

"Hey! What was that for?"

Smirking, she withdrew the half-full bottle of champagne from her purse.

"One for the road?"

"Don't mind if I do!"

Matthew leaned past Scarlet to retrieve two clean champagne flutes from the mini-bar area, and as he did so, he caught a whiff of her perfume. It was fresh and floral and subtle and made his head spin.

Scarlet poured the champagne and then held up her glass to toast.

"To crazy ideas."

Matthew smiled and held up his own glass.

"To crazy ideas… that just might work."

They toasted with a soft *clink*, then nervously sipped at their glasses as they cruised through the streets of Las Vegas. Before long, the limo slowed as Greg pulled up in front of the hotel where the gala was being held.

The party was already in full swing. A kind of trance-like electronic music filled the air with a low, driving bass line that you could almost feel moving through you. The lights in the ballroom were dimmed just enough to make you feel tipsy even if you hadn't been drinking, and the decorations were simple, classy, and of the highest quality. And oh! The guests.

To simply call the guests glamorous would be an unforgivable understatement. The ballroom was packed with well over a hundred of the best-dressed human beings Matthew had ever seen. Men and women ranging in age from early twenties to late seventies milled about making small talk and drinking glasses of wine that cost more than Matthew had spent on groceries in the last six months. The suits were tailored to perfection, the dresses flattered every curve, the jewelry and watches dazzled even in the low lighting.

Matthew probably would have stood in the ballroom entryway, stunned, all night were it not for Scarlet. Unfazed by the exorbitant wealth and culture surrounding her, she strode confidently into the room, leading Matthew by the hand to the table where they could pick up their name tags.

True to his word, Benny had gotten them onto the list. They picked up their tags, which were magnetic so as not to poke holes in anyone's $20,000 suit, and labeled themselves as deserving members of such a soiree. Once he'd made sure his name was perfectly level across his lapel, Matthew looked to Scarlet for guidance.

"What now?"

"I'm not sure. I've never done this before, remember?"

"I feel so out of place."

"Just try to own it. Pretend like you belong here. Fake it till you make it."

"Easier said than done."

"Let's start by getting some drinks. Then at least we'll have something to do with our hands."

"Good plan."

As they made their way across the crowded room, Matthew tried to figure out how to look like he belonged. He scanned the faces of the wealthy and well-dressed, sure that one of them would suddenly point him out and yell "Imposter!" Yet no one seemed to take any notice of the two young fashion industry wanna-bes. They made it safely to the drink table.

Scarlet ordered a bourbon on the rocks. Just like at the restaurant on their kinda-sorta date. Matthew, who was already a bit lightheaded from the combination of stress and champagne, stuck with a soda.

A server handed the pair their drinks, and they turned to face the sea of fashion-makers once more. They had barely taken two steps away from the table when a loud, familiar voice rang out.

"Son of Mark Kim! We meet at last!"

Matthew's head snapped in the direction of the voice. Benny Jenson, investor extraordinaire, heir to his late father Peter Jenson's exorbitant estate. Benny had an appearance to match his booming voice. Tall, thickly-built, red-faced, he embodied the stereotype of the powerful American white male. He covered the distance between them with just a few long strides, smiling broadly and extending a huge meaty hand to shake Matthew's.

Flustered, Matthew quickly moved his soda to his left hand so he could use his right to shake. He regretted having held the soda with his right, since now his handshake would be cold and clammy. Benny didn't seem to notice. He continued to grin at Matthew, with perfectly straight, white teeth.

"I was wondering when I might find you! Everything go okay with the limo?"

"Oh yes, thank you so much for arranging that! It was definitely a luxury after a life of taxis!"

"Not a problem, not a problem. I take it this lovely young lady is your business partner?"

"Yes, yes she is. Benny, allow me to introduce Ms. Scarlet Love. Scarlet, this is Benny Jenson."

Benny reached out to take Scarlet's hand, kissing the back of it ever so lightly in an old-fashioned and slightly uncomfortable display of chivalry. Scarlet flinched imperceptibly, but maintained her composure.

"It's a pleasure to meet you, Ms. Love."

"Please, call me Scarlet. And the pleasure's all mine."

"Scarlet it is. Some party, huh?"

"Definitely. Matthew and I are certainly feeling a little out of our depths here."

"Ah, don't let these old windbags intimidate you. Everyone had to get their start somewhere, right?"

"That's true. Maybe you could help us get ours? Are there any investor friends of yours you might be willing to introduce us to?"

"Sure! Anything for the son of Mark Kim and the lovely Ms. Love. Let's see…"

He scanned his eyes around the party, muttering names to himself as he did so.

"George and Betty are here somewhere, but I don't see them… Harriet doesn't like taking chances on new talent… Rodolfo is a possibility…"

As Benny contemplated his contacts, Scarlet nudged Matthew and nodded in the direction of an early-middle-aged Asian woman standing near the center of the room. She was not old, but her supreme confidence and cool gaze gave her the authority of a fearsome matriarch. The lines of her fitted black-and-white dress were angular and severe, fashionable and intimidating. Other guests seemed to flock to her, drawn like moths to a light. Matthew recognized her instantly from the notes Scarlet had prepared. It was Mary Chin.

Matthew was wondering how they might maneuver themselves to cross paths with the fashion industry icon, but as usual, Scarlet was one step ahead. Clearing her throat, she interrupted Benny's mumbled thoughts.

"Excuse me, um, Benny? You wouldn't happen to know Mary Chin by any chance, would you?"

Benny smirked, eager for the chance to show off his impressive network of friends.

"As a matter of fact, I do know her! She and I worked together last year on a spring show for some of the new designers we were considering. Great lady. Very tough. Very smart."

"That's what we've heard. She's had a lot of success with some pretty unique brands, right?"

"Yep, that's right. She's got the magic intuition for what's gonna hit it off next season like nobody else I've ever met. If a designer gets the Mary Chin stamp of approval, they're almost guaranteed to get support from the rest of the fashion world."

"Do you think... do you think you might be able to introduce us?"

Benny paused a moment. Clearly Ms. Chin's opinion meant enough to him that he did not want to risk his reputation associating with such an unproven and unlikely young business. After a long and awkward silence, he sighed.

"Ah, what the hell. I guess I wouldn't be where I am today if it weren't for Mr. Kim. I owe it to him to give his kid the same chance, right? I'll introduce you two. Just try not to embarrass me, okay?"

"We'll do our best."

Benny straightened his tie, as Matthew and Scarlet turned to one another to make final, last-minute adjustments to each other's outfits. Matthew's hands flittered lightly around the starburst design on Scarlet's dress in an attempt to perfect the angles of each detail, while Scarlet brushed nonexistent specks of dust or dandruff off of Matthew's shoulders. They then turned back to Benny.

"We're ready."

"Okay, follow me then."

When Matthew and Scarlet had crossed the ballroom alone, they may as well have been ghosts. No one looked at or acknowledged them in the slightest. Trying to get through the crowds while escorted by Benny, though, was a different story. They stopped every few feet so that Benny could exchange laughs with an old friend, or handshakes with an old business partner. Matthew was glad to know their ally had such a powerful reputation, but he was also growing more impatient with each small delay.

Finally they reached the outside of the circle of eager young people surrounding Mary Chin. With his huge frame and impressive status, Benny was able to slowly maneuver closer to the center of the circle, bringing Matthew and Scarlet along for the ride. At last they reached the legend herself. Benny flashed his winning smile and clasped one of Mary's small, bony hands between his two massive bear paws.

"Mary Chin, how have you been, my dear?"

"Benny Jenson! I thought I saw you earlier, but you disappeared before I could say hello. Not avoiding me, are you?"

"Never, my dear! It was an honest mistake, I promise. I could never intentionally miss an opportunity to talk to you."

"Well, I'm glad to hear it. Now are you going to introduce me to your friends here?"

"Yes, of course. Mary, this is Matthew Kim and Scarlet Love. They're business partners working on a fashion start-up specializing in 3D-printing. They're looking for some investors to help them get off the ground."

Mary narrowed her eyes, sizing up the pair.

"Interesting. And do either of you have any prior experience with starting a company?"

Matthew cleared his throat.

"Ahem, well, no, not exactly. This is our first endeavor, but we're pretty confident we can –"

Mary cut him off abruptly with a single raised hand.

"I'm sorry, young man, but unfortunately I don't have time for inexperience. I have a lot of highly qualified and established designers vying for limited resources. I'm sure you understand."

Matthew felt as if all of the air had been sucked out of his chest. His face was defeated and resigned. He started to turn around to get as far away as possible when Scarlet grabbed his arm, hard. Her face was livid, and she seemed to quiver with anger at the disrespect. When she spoke, the words came out in a snarl.

"Now you wait just one minute."

Mary's eyes widened, clearly taken aback.

"Excuse me?"

"You heard me. I realize you're a very busy and successful woman. But all we're asking for is five minutes of your time to present our business plan. Can you spare five minutes?"

Mary stared at Scarlet, sizing her up. Her face was unreadable. The tension was palpable and Matthew could feel himself start to sweat. Finally the intimidating fashionista spoke.

"All right. You may have five minutes."

Matthew was stunned. Scarlet took it all in stride, though, and wasted no time launching into an elevator pitch of the concept for their company, an overview of the business and marketing plan, and a summary of their fundraising efforts to date. Mary listened obediently throughout, nodding occasionally. But when Scarlet got to the details of their Kickstarter campaign, Mary became visibly more interested.

"You've raised thirty-four thousand dollars in less than five months? With no previous experience starting a company?"

Matthew had finally regained his composure and found his voice.

"That's correct, ma'am. We've had considerable success in working towards our fifty thousand dollar goal. I guess you could say we're pretty persistent salespeople."

"Yes, that much is quite clear," Mary said with a smirk in Scarlet's direction. "And you think that fifty would be enough to cover the costs of the 3D-printer, materials, a storefront, etc?"

"We believe so. The 3D-printed items are smaller accessories or accent features of our designs, so we won't be needing an industrial-scale printer until we're having some real commercial success, at which point we anticipate having the funds to procure one. In the meantime, we have obtained permissions from CalTech to continue using theirs to produce our prototypes."

"I see. And where might this business be based?"

"San Francisco. I live in the area, and I've already found a small storefront in the fashion district that we can use. It would be well under 100,000 bucks a year, but again, we'd hold off on starting a lease until we have a contract from a larger distributor to give ourselves a bit of a cushion."

"I think that's wise. And do you have distributors in mind already? Have you contacted them yet?"

"Actually, that's part of what we'd hoped to accomplish this weekend. We've just finished up our first batch of prototypes, including the items we're wearing." Matthew gestured down at his own suit, as well as Scarlet's dress. Mary raised one eyebrow, and Matthew thought she looked just a little bit impressed. "You were the investor we were most interested in speaking with, not just for your financial expertise, but for your connections to innovative design groups. We had hoped to take advantage of your network of distributors, who have already proven their success in selling unusual and unique designs."

"Interesting. Yes, I do have contacts among large-scale distributors who like to take chances on cutting-edge techniques. And you believe you can make this technology cost-efficient enough to convince them to take you on?"

Matthew and Scarlet smiled, exchanging glances. They'd crunched the numbers so many times they could have recited the calculations by heart. They knew exactly where they would have to make cuts and sacrifices, and how to optimize those decisions to maximize profit. Scarlet took a small step forward towards Mary, lowering her voice a bit.

"We would love to go over the numbers with you. Is there someplace quieter where we could go talk?"

Mary stared at the two grinning partners for a long minute, then turned wordlessly to exit the ballroom. She made a hooking motion with one finger as she turned, and Matthew and Scarlet scurried to follow the fashion legend.

Out in the lobby, Mary held a brief, hushed conversation with one of the hotel employees, who promptly led them to a small private conference room. Scarlet and Matthew sat down side-by-side, directly across from Mary. Mary had pulled from her purse a small notepad, a pen, and her reading glasses. She slid the stylish horn-rimmed glasses onto the bridge of her nose, picked up the pen, and raised her gaze to meet the pair sitting across from her.

"All right then. Let's talk business."

Chapter 41

The heavy door shut, and the conference room was silent except for the ticking of a large atomic clock on the wall. Matthew and Scarlet sat wordlessly, staring at the empty chair that Mary Chin had just vacated. Nearly a full minute passed, marked by the great clock's ticking, before Matthew realized that he was holding his breath. He released the air from his lungs in a heavy *whoosh*. The sound snapped Scarlet from her reverie. She turned toward him.

"Did that really just happen?"

"I… I'm still not sure."

"I think maybe it actually happened."

"I think maybe you're right."

"She actually *liked* us, Matthew."

"It would certainly appear so, yes."

"She liked us enough to invest."

"I remember."

"She liked us enough to *really* invest."

Matthew couldn't help but laugh.

"I remember. I was there too. Sixteen thousand dollars."

"Enough to meet our Kickstarter goal."

"Yeah. Fifty thousand dollars. Enough to produce an initial order. Which we could actually get with Mary's connections."

"Can you believe she's going to talk to Luke Rosenberg about distributing for us? It's all happening so fast."

"And with Mary on the team as a lead designer, there's no way he'll say no."

Scarlet sunk back into her chair, letting her head fall back and her eyes close. Matthew could relate to the feeling. It was as if, suddenly, an enormous weight had been lifted from their shoulders. They had the funding. This business was going to be a reality. The relief was not without a hint of fear, of apprehension at the great unknown that was the future. Even with Mary's guidance, there was no guarantee they would make it. And now, as they left their safe, stable careers and schooling to enter a new industry, they were completely and totally invested in the success or failure of the fledgling start-up. But still, this was a major victory. A huge vote of confidence in their ideas, and a very real sum of money to try and make their dreams a reality.

As they sat and basked in the afterglow of the deal, Matthew felt his smile grow wider and wider across his face. He nudged his business partner with his elbow. She opened one eye, saw his giddy smile, and broke into a grin herself. She sat back up in her chair.

"So, what do we do now?"

Matthew didn't have to think about it.

"That's easy. Now, we celebrate."

Taking Scarlet by the hand, he stood and led her out of the conference room, back to the party, straight to the bar.

"Two glasses of champagne, please."

The drinks appeared quickly, and Matthew raised his glass, fixated on the effervescent bubbles. Scarlet raised her own to meet his.

"To us?"

"To us."

As so often happened when Matthew consumed alcohol, the evening seemed to pass in a blur. But this time, it was a good blur. A whirlwind of happy sights and sounds, Scarlet's smiling face, friendly and well-dressed strangers.

The night ended with a good blur, too. Everything happened in a rush, but Matthew found himself back in the hotel room with Scarlet, watching the starburst dress slip smoothly over the curves of her hips. Only one of the two beds was used that night, and Matthew finally found out, once and for all, how his business partner felt about him.

Chapter 42

Year: 2018

"Aaaaaaand that concludes the first annual GEN SF fashion show, ladies and gentlemen! The first-ever show to feature holographic models! We've seen a wide range of pieces today, all of them unique and highly unconventional. This GEN SF line is clearly a design gamble, and only time will tell if there's enough public interest in these unusual 3D-printed styles for that gamble to pay off. Thanks so much for tuning in today, and as always, thanks for watching the Fashion Today channel. I'm Leroy Bloom, signing off."

As the trendy French house music began to play during the show's credits, Matthew spoke the command to turn off the television. He suddenly realized he hadn't taken a full breath since the show started. He released a long, heavy sigh, and turned to his business partner and wife.

"Well? What'd you think?"

Scarlet was lounging in the chocolate brown armchair beside his. The chairs had been the new couple's first home furnishing purchase after moving into their small but comfortable San Francisco apartment. She was still staring at the now black screen and was absentmindedly twisting the silver wedding band on her ring finger. She didn't appear to have heard him. Clearing his throat, Matthew tried again.

"Scar?"

"Hmm? What's that?"

"I was asking what you thought of the show."

"Well, I think that teal dress is still not falling as well as I'd like through the shoulders. It's bunching a bit."

"I still chalk that up to the holograms. They still don't move as smoothly as the human models. I think it causes some odd lines in a few of the pieces. But I meant what did you think of the whole thing?"

"I think... I think it's too early to say. It could really go either way. I'm not sure the industry is quite ready for our line. I think the public will buy if we can get some positive reviews… but I have no idea if that will happen."

"That's true. Maybe we should call Mary and see what she thought?"

"She's in Boston right now; she's probably busy with something."

"Nah, she wouldn't miss our first show."

Testing his theory, Matthew raised his voice to speak to the home entertainment and communication system.

"ECHO, please call Mary Chin."

A computerized woman's voice responded. "Calling Mary Chin."

The living room filled with the ringing sound of the outgoing call. After three rings, Matthew was starting to worry he'd been mistaken, but then Mary picked up.

"Hello there, Matthew."

"Hi Mary! You're on with Scarlet, as well."

"Scarlet, darling, how are you?"

"Hi Mary. I'll be better if you tell us you loved the show!"

There was a brief silence, and Scarlet glanced nervously at Matthew. He was chewing on one of his thumbnails. Finally their beloved investor and advisor spoke up again.

"You know I love your styles. I always have. But this was a very aggressive, ambitious line. And some of the biggest names in this industry do not like things that are aggressive and ambitious."

Matthew sniffed, still gnawing at his nail.

"So… what exactly does that mean for us?"

"Well, you'll need enough positive interest that you can generate the funds you need to expand into a major line. And what I'm seeing online is… not exactly positive."

"Already?!"

"The blogosphere never sleeps, darlings. I've just sent you some of the links. Try not to obsess. It's still early. This is only a tiny subset of the opinions we care about."

"We'll check them out, thanks."

"I mean it, Matthew. Don't stress just yet. I've seen companies bounce back from far worse reviews than these. Let's just wait for the rest of the verdicts to arrive, and we'll go from there."

"Okay. Thanks, Mary."

"Of course. Have a beautiful day, kids."

"Bye!"

A soft click, and the line went dead.

Matthew and Scarlet spent the next few hours poring through the opinions of countless members of the fashion community on the success or failure of their show. As Mary had warned, the reviews by many of the most well-established and traditional veterans of the fashion world were less than positive. At first, reading such negative opinions of their work was shocking and hurtful. As time passed, though, the pair began to grow immune to the harsh words, and even began to see the humor in some of the articles and blogs.

"Wait, I've got a good one here!" Scarlet gushed, fighting to hold back a wave of giggles. *"The organizers of the GEN SF show may have been striving for pageantry, but viewers found only a carnival-esque explosion of the extreme and the grotesque. In their quest to be different, GSF has blown way past unique and straight into the realm of uncalled-for."*

Matthew laughed so hard he accidentally spat out part of the tortilla chip he'd been eating.

"Oh yeah? How 'bout this one? *'It's been a long time since a fashion show has offended my sensibilities so severely that I was not inclined to keep watching. The GEN SF show earlier this afternoon illustrated the importance of having SOME kind of artistic qualifications if you wish to join the fashion industry. I don't attempt to do my accountant's job, and I don't expect him to attempt to do mine. It is high time for the novices at GEN SF to hang up their sketch pads and scurry back to the cubbies from which they came.'''*.

Scarlet wrinkled up her nose and crouched down, pretending to be a mouse. She made a show of scurrying around the living room, eliciting a new wave of laughter from Matthew. She collapsed back into her chair, panting from the exertion of her rodent antics. She was still smiling to herself when she glanced over at Matthew and realized he had stopped laughing. His face was dead serious as he stared at the glowing screen of his laptop.

"Hey, now, none of that. We agreed not to take these naysayers too seriously, remember?"

"It's not that. I think… I think I found a positive review!"

"No shit? What does it say?"

Matthew's hands were shaking a bit as he scrolled back to the top of the article. He cleared his throat weakly.

"There will surely be those who say that the fashion world is not ready for GEN SF. This small, spunky, San Francisco-based group specializes in eclectic, unusual, and even shocking 3D-printed designs and utilizes only biodegradable materials. It's true that the designs displayed by GEN SF would have no place in most traditional fashion shows. But that's because this line is not intended to simply be the latest in a long line of combinations of dresses, boots, and bags. No, this is something new entirely. This is an evolution in the field of fashion from pure aesthetics to high technology and social commentary. The pieces displayed in GEN SF's premier show earlier today are unapologetically different, unique, and striking. The designers have made bold use of unexpected colors in a manner that is reminiscent of Adelina Bianchi's work in the early twentieth century. The 3D-printing technique allows for the construction of new lightweight structures that would previously be impossible with simple textiles or plastic molds. And the environmental focus of the

company ensures that you are paying not just for high fashion, but for a commitment to leave the planet a better place than we found it. Take my word for it – GEN SF will be making waves in the world of fashion for years to come."

As he finished, Matthew looked up to gauge Scarlet's reaction. Her face was impossible to read. After a long moment, she smiled.

"Finally. *Someone* gets it."

"Looks like it."

"You're sure Mary didn't write that, right?"

Matthew chuckled and shook his head, scrolling through the author's bio.

"Nope, not Mary. It's a woman named Jasmine Watts. Apparently she's a well-known technology critic… but she's written up reviews and articles on fashion topics on occasion when she feels there's been a breakthrough in the materials or techniques being used. I guess she thinks we represent a breakthrough!"

"Well, I hope Jasmine has some like-minded friends. We could use a few more reviews like that."

As it turned out, Jasmine did have like-minded friends. Or at least, there existed a number of like-minded individuals. Over the next few days, as the reviews continued to emerge, the tide shifted in the direction of positive opinions. The reviews from experts in high technology were especially enthusiastic about the potential of the 3D-printing techniques, and writers on the topic of lifestyles gushed about the significance of a company that utilized eco-friendly and locally-sourced materials.

The young company even received some coverage on the local news, although mainly for their use of holographic models. Still, it was much-needed publicity. On the waves of the fashion show's success, Matthew began to reach out to venture capital firms to gauge their potential willingness to help fund some steps toward a major expansion, including construction of a large-scale dedicated production facility complete with their own industrial 3D printer, the hiring of additional designers and a marketing team, and a larger office space for the expanded team.

As GEN SF's reputation grew and improved, Matthew could sense the changing attitudes from the VC firms. Still, most were hesitant to commit the requested funds without stronger evidence of proven commercial success. Matthew was starting to wonder if they would ever be able to find the support for the expansion… until one day, about three weeks after the show, when the phone rang.

"Hello?"

"Hello. Is this Matthew Kim?"

The voice on the other end of the line was male, low and quiet. The English was clipped, with only the trace of an accent evident.

"Speaking. And who might this be?"

"My name is Sung-hoon Park. I'm a senior vice president at Jinhwa Technologies. Perhaps you've heard of us."

Matthew could hear the smile in Park's voice. Jinhwa Tech was a Korean company, a giant in the technology industry, with a hand in most of the major electronics developments of the last ten years. They were also known for engineering the latest generation of 3D-printers. The Jinhwa printers were lighter, faster, and more versatile than anything else on the market. They were also well outside the price range of GEN SF.

"I've definitely heard of you. How can I help you, Mr. Park?"

"Well, you'll be receiving the formal details in writing by the end of the day, but I wanted to speak with you ahead of time so you aren't blindsided."

"And what exactly would I be blindsided by?"

"Mr. Kim, I'm calling to inform you that Jinhwa Technologies is interested in acquiring GEN SF."

Chapter 43

"C'mon, Matthew, spit it out."

Scarlet had her arms crossed over her chest, and was tapping one foot impatiently on the kitchen floor. Across the table, Matthew was squirming from the exertion of holding in the news of the phone call. He'd called Scarlet immediately after hanging up with the Jinhwa executive, but only to tell her that he had news, and that they could discuss it over dinner. She had been running errands at the time, and now that two hours had elapsed she was starting to grow irritated with the suspense. She hadn't even looked twice at the veritable feast of veal marsala, spinach salad, and grilled asparagus Matthew had prepared.

"Tell me before I hurt you." From the dangerous glint in her eye, Matthew knew better than to push his luck any longer.

"Okay, fine. We got an offer today."

"An offer? What kind of offer?"

"An acquisition offer."

Scarlet fell back in her chair, letting out a long breath through her teeth. It was big news. But not necessarily the best of news.

"From who?"

"Jinhwa Technologies. The Korean technology giant."

"I know who they are. Wow… That's a pretty major group."

"Yeah."

"Remember back when we were getting started and we did all that research on 3D-printers? Their machines are miles better than the competition."

"I remember. They also cost three times as much."

"I guess it makes sense that they'd be interested in us because of our printed designs."

"Yeah. That's what Mr. Park – the Jinhwa exec who called me – said, anyway. Apparently they've been pushing pretty hard recently to pick up smaller companies who are using 3D-printing technologies in new ways. If they can take all these new ideas and apply their superior machines, they could pretty quickly expand into all sorts of new markets."

"I can imagine. So, moment of truth. What's the offer?"

"Well, Park said things would be open to a little negotiation… but the gist of the offer was 9.2 million. They'd employ us to run the day-to-day operations, along with a small team of our choosing for design purposes. We'd be able to take advantage of Jinhwa's existing production and marketing resources. And of course, access to as many Jinhwa printers as we need."

"Nine-point-two million? Wow. That's a pretty generous offer."

"Exceedingly so. I actually said that to Park. He said maybe we shouldn't mention that in negotiations," Matthew said with a laugh. "But he also said it's a cost they're more than willing to pay to get a strong foothold in a brand new industry. They've never done anything with fashion applications before."

"I'd hardly call ours a strong foothold, but I won't complain about someone offering us north of nine million bucks."

"I'm in the same place. So now it's time to talk." Matthew leaned back and rubbed his temples. "Is this what we want to do?"

"Let's pro-con this sucker. Pro: we're guaranteed funding for our expansion plan."

"Pro: we'd have guidance from people with actual expertise running and building businesses. Less opportunities for us to mess everything up."

"But where's the fun in that?" Scarlet asked, a mischievous smile playing at the corners of her mouth. "Pro: secure salaries, even if a line doesn't do too well right off the bat."

"Which means a much lower chance of being homeless at some point in the next few years," Matthew responded, his face considerably less joking and more concerned than his wife's. "Pro: huge potential customer base. Jinhwa is a household name, and their marketing team is unparalleled."

"Pro: access to those *sweet* printers of theirs without paying a fortune. We could really amp up the complexity of the designs if we didn't have to worry about cost. Plus, productivity would skyrocket with a whole army of printers working at once, not to mention the rest of their facilities."

There was a short silence as Matthew tried to think of another major advantage of taking the Jinhwa offer. "I think we've hit the biggest pros. Con time?"

"Sure. Con: I don't think the Jinhwa big-wigs would like us very much."

Matthew cocked his head to one side. "Why's that? Mr. Park seemed nice enough on the phone earlier."

"Well, think about that corporate culture. It's massive, super-efficient, impersonal, and rigidly planned and executed. You and me, on the other hand… we take risks and make mistakes, hit a lot of roadblocks, and generally don't really know what we're doing. I imagine their patience with us would run thin pretty quickly."

"I hadn't thought about that… but it's a good point. I wonder if our inexperience would frustrate them to the point of trying to relieve us of some of our operational authorities."

"I wouldn't be surprised. I think the tech industry in general is like that. If you're not qualified or competent enough to do your job as well as somebody else, step aside and let them do it."

"Which is great, in theory. Just not when it's our company and we're the incompetent ones." Matthew laughed uncomfortably.

Scarlet was quiet then, staring down at the table full of steaming, aromatic food without really seeing any of it. When she met Matthew's eyes again, she had a strange look on her face.

"You know… I realize it's crazy… but I don't really want to sell the company."

Matthew sighed his relief.

"Me neither. But I don't know how we could justify not taking this offer. It's just so much money."

"It's *so* much money. But I mean… if we decide we don't want to become part of Jinhwa, there are other ways of raising the money for our expansion project."

"I'm listening."

"Well… I've been thinking for a while about what we might be able to do… and I was thinking that maybe an IPO would work well for us?"

Matthew nodded thoughtfully, considering Scarlet's words. Taking the company public was certainly a very different path to funding. There would be more risks, more challenges than simply taking the Jinhwa offer. But then again, as Scarlet had pointed out earlier, facing risks and challenges was kind of their style.

Matthew began to serve himself food from the dishes on the table, gesturing for Scarlet to do the same.

"Dinner's going to get cold if we wait until we've discussed every option." Scarlet nodded and began serving herself as well. "I think you could be on to something with the IPO thing, though."

Scarlet nodded enthusiastically.

"We could still raise money quickly. Maybe not nine million dollars, but I bet we could raise enough to get the expansion plan off the ground pretty quickly and really step up our game."

"And all without worrying about fitting in with a bunch of suit-wearing tech geeks."

"No one to kick us out if they don't like how we run our business."

"It would also get our name out there and hopefully help spread our brand, improve the public image and recognition."

"Definitely a risk, though." Matthew couldn't help but feel the familiar twist in his gut that always accompanied uncertainty and change in his life.

In contrast, Scarlet's eyes were liquid emerald fire. They burned with a fearless spirit, full of optimism for the future.

"Anything worth having is worth fighting for," she said. "Besides, what's life without a little risk?"

Her fire was contagious, and a grin began to spread across Matthew's face. He was reminded yet again of how lucky he was to have found this spunky, inspiring, courageous woman. And even luckier, that he'd been able to convince her to marry him. He reached across the table to place his right hand over her left. She twisted her thumb to hook it around his. Even after four years together, Matthew still felt butterflies in his stomach.

"You're right," he said, feeling giddy with excitement, with romance, with the rush of living life. "Let's do this."

Chapter 44

The next day, it was Matthew's task to return Mr. Park's call and turn down the Jinhwa acquisition offer. Scarlet had already left for the office by the time he picked up the phone, and he was feeling a bit less confident without her irresistible self-assurance. His head spun as he considered the sheer enormity of 9.2 million dollars. The businessman in him knew that GEN SF had the potential to be worth even more down the line, with their continued hard work and a few lucky breaks. But those breaks were far from guaranteed. And even after four years in the fashion business, he still often felt like he had no idea what he was doing.

Suddenly, Adelina Bianchi's face floated into his mind. Her warm yet intense brown eyes, her shiny black hair styled to perfection, a knowing smile tugging at the corners of her lips. Then her voice was in his ear.

No one knows what they're doing, darling. That's the adventure.

Matthew blinked, and Biani's face faded away. He shivered, feeling as if he'd just seen a ghost. But it was a good feeling, seeing the ghost of a long-lost friend. Even as her image disappeared from view, her voice continued.

Don't cripple yourself. Stay hungry, stay ambitious, and the sky's the limit.

Matthew smiled, feeling his confidence return. He dialed Mr. Park's number, imbued by Biani's courage and Scarlet's determination, and turned down the acquisition offer that could have made him a rich man for the rest of his life. Mr. Park seemed more than a little surprised by the rejection, but maintained his cool, courteous tone. After they hung up, Matthew's next call was to Scarlet.

"Hey, babe." Scarlet sounded far-off and distracted.

"Hi. Just got off the phone with Mr. Park at Jinhwa."

"Yeah? How'd he take it?"

"I think he thinks we're idiots," Matthew said with a laugh. "Which we probably are."

"Maybe so. But I think I'm okay with that."

"Good. I'm okay with it too. What are you up to right now?"

"I'm in the lab. The new PLA blend isn't solidifying as quickly as it should be. Could be an issue with the binder. I'm trying to troubleshoot."

"Okay, well I'll let you get back to it. You sound distracted. I'll be into the office shortly."

"Great, see you soon. Love you."

"Love you too. Bye!"

Matthew hung up, and quickly finished getting dressed for work. He slung his messenger bag over one shoulder, grabbed his bike, and bounced down the apartment steps and onto the city streets. He stopped briefly at his favorite mural, painted on the side of an abandoned shop at the end of his street. It depicted three young teenagers, two girls and a boy, painting the skyline of San Francisco on a large white canvas. Below the mural was a quote from author William Saroyan, which stated: "San Francisco itself is art, above all literary art. Every block is a short story, every hill a novel. Every home a poem, every dweller within immortal. That is the whole truth."

Matthew stood for a moment and smiled at the mural, as he did every morning, then headed north towards the GEN SF storefront. They'd recently purchased an office space above the storefront, where they'd placed a small, personal-use 3D printer, as well as a number of desk spaces for design work and business administration. They used the in-office printer for testing out new designs and prototypes, and then took advantage of the CalTech printer for large-scale production when necessary. However, with Scarlet's CalTech friends quickly finishing up their PhDs, she wasn't sure how much longer they would be able to access the university's equipment, adding extra pressure to fund the expansion plan in the near future.

Matthew biked along at a leisurely pace, in no great hurry to get to work. He enjoyed his time there, of course, but the recent push for funding had also made it stressful and demanding. He knew taking the company public would be a huge undertaking, and wondered once again if they'd made a mistake in turning down Jinhwa. In order to achieve any kind of success with the IPO, Matthew thought, they needed another big win, and quickly. Something to boost both capital and moral, and show the fashion world that they were a force to be reckoned with, rather than a young company with a few lucky breaks.

But how? If there was one thing Matthew truly hated about the fashion industry, it was the fact that it didn't always reward hard work. All his life, he'd done well for himself simply by dogged perseverance and tireless effort. Even if he lacked skill, he was the hardest worker in the classroom or office. But with fashion, you couldn't muscle your way to a successful line. It took creativity, inspiration, and genuine ability to make real something that had never existed before. A big hit with a brand new design line could be just what they needed to gain the momentum for an IPO, but force of will alone wouldn't be enough to make such a line a reality.

Matthew gently squeezed the handbrake as he approached a red light. He felt suddenly overwhelmed by the task of new design work. He felt as if he had the designer's equivalent of writer's block – no matter how hard he tried, he couldn't make the new ideas come. Somewhere in the corner of his mind he heard the tapping of a heeled shoe against a wooden floor. He blinked, and when he opened his eyes the apparition of Adelina Bianchi was floating before him for the second time that day. This time she looked a bit annoyed.

Don't sell yourself short, Matthew. You're more talented than you realize.

Thankfully he was still stopped at the light, because Matthew nearly fell off his bike at the sudden appearance of his old friend. He quickly swung his leg over and walked the bike off the road to gather himself before he got run over by the rush hour traffic. He crossed the sidewalk to stand with his back against a brick storefront, catching his breath. He stared hard at the image of the long-dead designer, which to passers-by was simply empty air beside the "No Parking" sign.

"What is it?" Matthew muttered under his breath to the floating hallucination. "What am I supposed to do?"

Biani's ghost said nothing, but narrowed her eyes. Matthew grew frustrated.

"What do you want me to do?" He raised his voice a bit, eliciting stares from a hipster-looking couple passing by on roller blades.

Don't be afraid of failure. Be persistently creative. What you do is an art, not a science.

And then she was gone, vanished into the warm San Francisco morning without a trace. Matthew stood for a moment while her words settled in and took up residence somewhere in his chest. Slowly, the words formed a spark. The spark spread gradually through his body until it had become a feeling. An inspiration. And then, Matthew knew

what to do. He got back on his bike and raced to the office.

Chapter 45

Matthew nearly tripped over his own feet in his eagerness to get up the stairs to the office. He burst in with sweat stains on his shirt from his hard ride through the city, instantly searching for Scarlet. The newest employee, a young marketing representative named Tommy, looked up at Matthew nervously from beneath his long, sandy brown hair.

"Is everything alright, Mr. Kim?"

"You know, Tommy, I think it might be okay, yeah."

"Um... Can I help you with anything, sir?"

"You could point me in the direction of my beautiful wife, for a start."

Tommy turned and gestured in the direction of the back room where the prototype 3D-printer was located. Of course, Matthew remembered, she was still working with the troublesome PLA blend samples. He crossed the office in a flash and knocked open the door to the back room with a bit more force than was necessary. Scarlet was hunched over the table on which the printer rested, apparently trying to peer inside the cartridge containing the new polymer blend, as if seeing the powdery mixture might help her understand the issue. Her olive green shirt made her eyes sparkle like twin emeralds. She glanced up from the printer when Matthew bust into the room.

"Hey. You startled me."

"Sorry about that. I'm in a good mood."

"I wish I could say the same. Why so cheery?"

"Because I had an idea."

"Oh?"

"Well, I guess it wasn't exactly my idea. It was Adelina's. But she shared it with me."

"Adelina? Adelina… *Bianchi*?" Scarlet's eyes narrowed and she lowered her voice. "Matthew, you didn't do that… that weird… time travel-y thing again, did you?"

Matthew laughed impatiently and shook his head.

"No, no, nothing like that. Or maybe just a little like that. It was more like a vision. But that's not the point. The important thing is that this vision gave me the inspiration for our next line."

"Go on..." Scarlet was still eyeing him suspiciously, as if he were a mental patient who had recently made the decision to go off his medication.

"I can't explain it here. Not enough space. Follow me." He turned on his heel and swept out of the room. Scarlet hesitated a moment, then followed him into the office. He was waiting for her with two bike helmets in his hands, his and hers. She stood and stared at her more-eccentric-than-usual husband.

"Matthew? What are you doing?"

"C'mon. We're going for a ride. Like I said, not enough space in here."

Scarlet stared at him, puzzled. She was aware of the fact that Tommy and the two other employees in the office,

133

Linda the design assistant and Jorge the PR account coordinator, were all equally confused by their boss's behavior, though they were doing their best not to openly stare. Matthew didn't seem to notice, though. He was visibly antsy, rocking back and forth and his toes and gesturing with the two helmets for Scarlet to follow him.

"C'mon, Scar! I promise I'm not crazy. I really do have an idea."

Scarlet rolled her eyes. She hated to leave the office before she had resolved the PLA blend issues, but maybe a change of scenery was just what she needed. She crossed the floor to Matthew and grabbed her helmet from him.

"All right, let's go."

Matthew led the way downstairs and out the back door to the bike rack where the staff of GEN SF all stored their rides. He and Scarlet unlocked their bikes, both black Schwinns, snapped on their helmets, and set off. They headed north, with Scarlet following about half a length behind

Matthew. At first, she was agitated, eager to know where they were headed and why this trip had had to happen right away. But it was a beautiful day, sunny and warm and breezy, and she soon forgot all about the reason for the excursion and simply enjoyed the ride.

It was almost 10:00 AM, and most of the rush hour traffic had died down. They made it out of the Union Square shopping district with relative ease, and cruised all the way to North Beach so that they could continue their ride along the coast. Matthew slowed the pace as they traveled west along the northernmost edge of the city, watching the sun glinting off the bay and the gentle waves lapping softly at the boats moored in the marinas.

They rolled past the impressive status symbols bobbing in the Yacht Harbor, and past the spacious openness of Marina Green Park, where a few construction workers on break were kicking around a soccer ball. When they reached the green expanses of Crissy Field, where crowds of tourists sunbathed and picnicked in the shadow of the Golden Gate Bridge, Matthew slowed to a stop. He stepped off his bike and laid it down, then sat down and lay back with his arms spread, as if trying to make a snow angel. Scarlet followed his example, collapsing in the soft, sun-warmed grass. They both panted softly, a bit winded from the long ride in the growing midday heat.

For a while, the business-partners-turned-life-partners simply enjoyed the feeling of the sun on their faces. It was a full five minutes before Scarlet remembered the reason for their adventure. She rolled onto one side to face Matthew, who still had his eyes closed.

"So, is this enough space?"

"Hmm?"

"Is this enough space for you to tell me about your idea?"

"Oh! Right. Yes, this is perfect."

"Well?"

Matthew pushed himself up off of the soft grass to sit cross-legged. Scarlet mirrored him, sitting up so that their eyes were level.

"Okay," Matthew began. "So we decided not to take the Jinhwa offer."

"Correct."

"And we have this plan for an IPO."

"Also correct…"

"But we know that won't be easy."

Scarlet scoffed. "That's putting it mildly. There's a very good chance we'll fall on our faces."

"Exactly. We're not prepared right now to go public. We need to have a stronger foothold first. We need to make a statement."

"I think that makes sense."

"So, I've been thinking we need to release a new line."

Scarlet was quiet for a moment.

"Well, that's always the goal, Matthew. The whole design staff has been busting their asses lately. But the ideas just aren't flowing right now."

"I know, I know. And that's totally understandable, especially after we pulled out all the stops for the holographic show. But that's what I wanted to tell you."

"What? That we need to keep doing our jobs?"

"No. That I have an idea for the new line."

"An idea as in… a design?"

"More than that. A theme. A concept. A basis that we can use for all the designs in the line."

Scarlet grinned, finding her husband's enthusiasm contagious.

"Okay, hit me."

Matthew stood up and spread his arms wide to gesture towards their surroundings.

"This. This is our theme. This city."

Scarlet climbed to her feet and took in her surroundings. To her right and left were the picnickers on Crissy Field. People of every age and ethnicity imaginable, all intermingling on the bright emerald lawn. Eating, talking, laughing, dancing, snapping pictures. Locals and tourists alike took advantage of the beautiful weather to enjoy the sights of the San Francisco Bay.

And what a day to enjoy the Bay it was. Directly in front of Scarlet was the sparkling azure water, stretching out in different directions like a sprawling blue giant. Small boats with sails as white as driven snow bobbed effortlessly along in the lazy mid-morning breeze, while intrepid orange and red and yellow kayaks zigged and zagged their way through the gentle rippling wake.

And then there was the most noticeable feature in view. The Golden Gate Bridge loomed large and magnificent from up this close. It soared high above the sea level expanse of the field, its iconic red towers seeming to reach right up to

139

the fluffy white clouds above. The famous suspension bridge was one of Scarlet's favorite sights of all time, and something about it made her stomach do a little somersault. It was simply amazing what the human mind could come up with.

Scarlet soaked up her surroundings with intent focus. It didn't take long for her to begin to see the potential in Matthew's idea. She turned back to him with a smile slowly spreading across her face.

"Fashion inspired by San Francisco. I like it."

Matthew grinned, thrilled to have her approval.

"You sure? You think we can make it work?"

"Absolutely."

Scarlet dropped quickly to the ground to pick up her bike. She snapped her helmet back on and swung one leg over the bike, then motioned for Matthew to follow.

"C'mon!"

"Where are you going?"

"This line isn't going to design itself, silly. Let's get back to work!"

Matthew Kim didn't need to be told twice. He hopped on his bike and sped towards the office.

Chapter 46

For the next few weeks, the office was a blur of activity. Scarlet had decided to hand out sketchbooks to every member of GEN SF, even those with no training or experience in design work.

"It doesn't have to be beautiful, or polished," she told the confused bunch of employees. "The design team will be responsible for the final products. But what we need right now are ideas, and lots of them. Let the city inspire you!"

And so they did. Matthew and Scarlet collected the sketchbooks each week. There was a minimum quota of five new ideas or designs. One quiet employee, a young man named Felipe who helped manage the storefront downstairs, showed such creativity and promise in his sketches each week that Scarlet decided he needed to be transferred to the design team immediately, to help full-time with the hunt for new ideas.

After each weekly sketchbook collection, Matthew and Scarlet pored over each fledgling design to decide which ones merited further refinement. Sometimes they took the design as it stood, and other times they picked out just the strongest elements for use in a different context. It was exhausting work, but much more conducive to creativity than simply staring at a blank page for hours on end, willing one's own brain to produce more big ideas.

As the some of the sketches came to look more and more like finished designs, Scarlet switched gears to focus more exclusively on the production of the pieces, while Matthew continued to select and enhance the drafts from the employee sketchbooks. On the production side of the office, Scarlet spent all day in the room with the 3D-printer, prototyping accent features and small but unusual accessories. In the room next door, the brother-sister seamstress duo of Jamie and Louise ran sewing machines constantly, piecing together the bulk material of the soon-to-be new pieces.

Matthew and Scarlet continued their system of crowd-sourcing ideas until they had settled on twelve strong designs to make up the new collection. Of these, six would be available in multiple colors, for eighteen total items. These eighteen pieces made up the display that they showed Mary Chin when she came in to evaluate the potential of GEN SF's pending new release.

The designs hung on mannequins, arranged in a semicircle in the center of the office. The world-renowned angel investor made her way slowly around the arc, stopping at each mannequin to observe how the garments fell over the curves of shoulders or hips, to feel the textiles used, or to evaluate the quality of clasps or buttons.

The collection was simply titled "Wear the City". Among Matthew's favorite items were two of the men's pieces. One was an old-fashioned silk top hat, available in black or cobalt grey, with a shiny silver hat band. The hat featured a 3D-printed cable car that ran along a track orbiting the hat from the brim to the crown, powered by a tiny eco-friendly battery within the car. Matthew's other favorite piece was a modern dinner jacket, in deep navy blue. Over the blue of the jacket was a layer of patterning depicting the "Painted Ladies," San Francisco's Victorian-era houses bearing many colors of paint to highlight different details of the structures. The pattern layer was thin enough that these colorful houses appeared more like a shadow, an idea just on the edge of consciousness. You could see the different tints and shades if you focused on them, but they could just as easily fade into the background.

A similar piece to the Painted Ladies jacket was available as a women's design. The women's jacket also came in navy blue, but was patterned all over with images of Alcatraz Island. The inside of the prison was not featured, as they hadn't wanted the jacket to be depressing or disturbing. The jacket displayed the island itself and the outline of the fortress-like prison, once again in a patterning layer so thin and sheer that you might miss it if you didn't pay attention. Scarlet loved that piece, claiming it made her feel powerful and proud.

Of course, Scarlet's favorite item in the collection was the one that celebrated her favorite sight in the city. It was a sleek A-line dress, the fabric a dizzying swirl of white and sky blue. Over this fabric were 3D-printed replicas of the Golden Gate Bridge towers, laid flat against the dress so that they rose only about half an inch above the surface. Connecting the iconic red towers were 3D-printed suspension cables, which were fastened to the dress only at their ends, so that the cables could sway a bit as the wearer moved. There were three complete miniature replicas of the bridge in total, each seeming to pierce the sunny sky of the dress.

Mary Chin did not speak a word during her analysis of the new collection. She occasionally hummed softly to herself as she let her fingers brush against the designs, but gave no indication as to her thoughts until she had completed the evaluation. At that time, she turned to Matthew and Scarlet, who were anxiously waiting at the back of the room, to give Mary space for her thoughts.

"Come back over here, you two."

They did as they were told, coming to stand beside the half-circle of mannequins as if they too were ready to be judged. Mary smiled.

"I like this collection. I like it a lot."

Matthew let his breath rush out in a relieved sigh.

"Really? Do you think it will sell?"

"I do. You two have maintained your very unique style here, but the images are so well-known and picturesque that they'll appeal to a broad consumer base. I think you can really have some success with this one."

Scarlet beamed. "I sure hope you're right about that."

And, as she so often was, Mary Chin was right. Young Tommy's marketing campaign was quite successful, with the promotional video he'd made going viral within hours of its release, thanks to the buzz he'd created on various social media sites in the days preceding. Soon after the video took off, so did traffic on the GEN SF website. Jorge worked tirelessly to secure contracts with a few different retailers to whom they could wholesale the collection, in addition to selling the line out of their own storefront. Scarlet wrote up a quick press release for the local newspapers about the new collection, as well.

Sales took off in a big way, both online and in different retail outlets. In the first month after the release of Wear the City, the revenue generated more than quadrupled what the previous collection, featured in the holographic fashion show, had produced in the same time. One night, a few months after the release, with sales still as strong as ever, Matthew rolled over in bed to face his wife.

"Are you awake?" He whispered softly.

"I am. What's up?" Scarlet's eyes were closed, and her voice was soft but alert. He hadn't woken her up.

"I've been thinking that maybe we're ready."

"Ready for what, Matthew?"

"For the IPO."

Now Scarlet opened her eyes. The corners of her mouth twitched as she fought back a smile. "Oh yeah?"

"Yeah. We're growing very quickly, generating a lot of revenue, and our market is big and getting bigger every day. We have a strong customer base and good relations with a number of different retailers. So we're not particularly vulnerable to risk. It seems like the right time to me. Am I just being impatient?"

Now Scarlet couldn't restrain the smile anymore. "I don't think you're impatient. I think you're smart. I think now is the perfect time."

"You know there's still a chance it could all fall apart, right?"

"I'm not worried about it."

"But if it all goes to hell, we'd lose everything."

"Not everything. No matter what happens with this company, we wouldn't lose everything. We've got each other. And that's all we need."

Matthew felt a warm feeling spread through his very core, and he slipped into the deepest, most rejuvenating night's sleep of his life.

Chapter 47

It was exactly 6:30 AM on the west coast when the NASDAQ opened on GEN SF's IPO day. In the first two hours of trading, the price of GSF stock dropped steadily. Alarmed, one of the newer employees called Matthew and Scarlet at home to ask whether they should be concerned about the decline.

The unorthodox business owners were still in bed when the office called at 8:00. Scarlet was less than enthusiastic about the wake-up call. She picked up after three rings.

"Hello."

"Ms. Love? This is Tommy. Tommy Jonas?"

Scarlet had kept her maiden name when they got married. She and Matthew had decided that for business reasons, it was best if they presented themselves to new clients and investors as business partners rather than life partners. That was easier when they had different last names.

"What do you want, Tommy? It's early."

"I know, and I apologize for calling at home, but I was just wondering if you and Mr. Kim were watching the trading?"

"We've been watching the back of our eyelids, Tommy."

"So sorry, Ms. Love. It's just that, well, GSF stock is already selling for almost 20% less than when we opened this morning."

Scarlet didn't say anything. Nervously, Tommy piped up again.

"Um… Ms. Love?"

"So what?"

"Excuse me?"

"So what? There isn't much we can do about it right this minute. Stocks go up and down, Tommy."

"I know, but –"

"Look, I know it can be stressful to see the numbers drop. But have a little faith. It's early. We aren't even two hours into day one yet. My advice to you is to stop watching the numbers. Go eat some breakfast. Take a shower. Go for a walk."

"Yes ma'am. Thank you, Ms. Love."

"Oh, and Tommy?"

"Yes, Ms. Love?"

"Unless the office is on fire or there are coyotes actively trying to eat you, don't ever call us at home again."

There was a brief silence on the line before Tommy responded, sheepishly.

"Yes, Ms. Love. Sorry to bother. Have a nice day."

"Good bye, Tommy."

As it turned out, Scarlet was right not to worry. Not long after her conversation with Tommy, the tide began to turn in their favor. The price of GSF stock slowly started to climb, and by 11:00 was more than 10 percent higher than at the start of trading. Matthew and Scarlet checked on the market only once during that time. They watched long enough to see that the stock was trending upward, then walked away. Of course they wanted to stay glued to the computer screen, watching every tiny tick up or down in the price of the stock that had the potential to help turn their tiny start-up into a big-time business. But they knew that obsessing wouldn't change the outcome of the trading.

And so, while the rest of GEN SF's employees and investors anxiously followed the stock's price movement over the course of the day, the young company's owners instead made lunch plans with Luke Rosenberg and Mary Chin at Luke's favorite Mexican restaurant.

The foursome convened at El Adobe just after 1:00 PM. At Luke's recommendation, they ordered chicken enchiladas, chips and guacamole, and margaritas for the table.

While they waited for the food to arrive, Mary interlaced her fingers and leaned forward across the table.

"So, have you two been stalking the NASDAQ all day?"

Matthew glanced at Scarlet and chuckled.

"Actually, no. We decided ahead of time that we didn't want this to be a cause for anxiety. Stocks go up and down. It's a volatile market. No reason to read meaning into every little dip and rise throughout the day. What happens, happens."

Luke shook his head, incredulous.

"I gotta say, guys, you two are not like any other business owners I've ever met. Please don't take offense... but you guys are weird."

Scarlet beamed. She certainly didn't seem to take offense. After all, she was an ex-engineer. Weird was pretty much a compliment.

Mary reached into her purse and pulled out a magazine, setting it on the table in front of Matthew and Scarlet. It was a British tabloid called *The Latest*.

"Speaking of weird…" Mary said as she flipped through the magazine to an article she had dog-eared. "Take a look at this."

The article was titled "Fashion's Most Unlikely Duo", and it featured a full-page picture of Matthew and Scarlet at a recent industry gala, sitting side-by-side at a round table filled with other fashion bigwigs. The married partners didn't look happy. They appeared to be bickering about something.

"Oh, well that's flattering," Scarlet said with a sarcastic smirk.

"Was this the Chicago thing a couple months back?" Matthew asked.

"Yeah, it looks like it. I don't think I've had those shoes more than a few months."

"What in the world are we arguing about here?"

"Chicago… Hmm… Oh! This is when we were trying to decide what color to paint the living room. You thought beige would work with the brown armchairs and I thought blue would add some life to the room."

"I think you're absolutely right. God, we battled over that stupid paint."

Luke was grinning.

"So what color did you end up choosing?"

Scarlet turned to face Luke.

"Forest green."

Luke looked confused.

"That wasn't one of the options?"

"Nope. But we've learned that sometimes it's better if fights don't have a winner and a loser."

Luke nodded slowly, and he and Mary exchanged smiles. They had discussed their opinions of the "unlikely duo" many times before. No matter how long they knew the couple, they never ceased to surprise and amuse.

The foursome continued to laugh and enjoy their enchiladas for over two hours. There was no more mention of stocks or money matters, simply jokes and stories and conversation among friends until the afternoon sun hung low over the San Francisco skyline.

[End... for now]

Epilogue – Year 2045

Elsa Kim rubbed at her eyes, which had become dry after another long day in the lab. It was a slow Thursday afternoon, and Elsa's labmates looked just as sleepy and uninterested as she did, leaning heavily on their elbows on the lab benches and staring into space, lulled nearly to sleep by the low, soothing hum of the machines. *What a lively bunch*, Elsa thought to herself with a bemused smile. *We may supposedly be on the cutting edge of technology, but you sure wouldn't know it to look at us.*

Elsa's lab was a small subsection of MIT's Physics PhD program that focused specifically on special applications of Einstein's theory of relativity. Although in recent years, there had been only one application that had achieved any success. And that was time travel. After being considered an impossibility for many years, the breakthrough in time travel technology had come in 2037, when researchers at CERN, in Switzerland, had discovered a way to stabilize wormholes. Without the problem of wormhole collapse, the research floodgates opened, quickly creating many thousands of links to different points in space-time.

The CERN breakthrough had taken place while Elsa was just starting her senior year in high school. She was so enthralled by the possibility of time travel that she quickly dropped her longstanding plan of becoming a fashion designer like her parents to pursue a degree in quantum physics. She'd been worried that Mom and Dad would be disappointed in her decision not to go into the family business, GEN SF, but they were surprisingly excited for her to make her own path in the world. Her father, especially, seemed just as enthusiastic as she was about the potential uses for time travel.

It was amazing to think that what had been considered impossible just eight years ago was rapidly approaching ordinary. The technology wasn't commonplace, per se, since the organizations and commissions governing its use had strict regulations on who could travel through time in order to avoid altering the course of human history. But it had been so thoroughly tested, explored, and publicized that Elsa's labs' findings would hardly be considered front-page news. In fact, even Elsa herself had time traveled, not long after starting her PhD studies at MIT in 2042. The professor who oversaw her lab had secured permissions for each of the lab's nine full-time researchers to accompany him on a trip to the year 2040. It was much easier to get permits for travel to dates post-2037, since contact with people before the advent of wormhole stabilizers could very feasibly induce hysteria.

When Elsa took place on that expedition in 2042, the technology was still full of glitches. For one thing, users often arrived at their destination time with an inexplicable fever, a phenomenon known colloquially as "time-sick". Nowadays, time-sickness had been all but eradicated. With the latest innovations, users were safely rendered unconscious for the entirety of wormhole travel, waking up healthy and comfortable, albeit a bit disoriented, in their destination time.

"Hey Elsa, your Ruby Ring is done. What a gorgeous gift for your parents!"

The sound of Jessica's voice snapped Elsa out of her near-comatose state.!! She snapped her eyes up to where her fellow grad student and best girl friend was standing, in the far corner of the lab beside a large metal machine that was powering down with a soft *whir*. She had inherited her father's jet black hair and golden skin, and her mother's bright green eyes and long, thin legs.

Elsa grinned, crossing the floor in a few graceful steps. The ruby ring's wonder starts today in 2042, a fortuitous invention completely unknown to Matthew and Scarlet in 2013.

ABOUT THE AUTHORS

Occy Yang is a businessman and attorney in Seattle, Washington. When not practicing business or real estate law, Occy spends his time on producing novels and designing card games. Occy always wanted to write an entertaining story that celebrates America's entrepreneurial generation. He also believes such entrepreneurship increases social mobility and diversity in this great nation. Occy holds a BA from Dartmouth College, an MBA from INSEAD in France, a JD from Cornell Law School, and an MPP from Harvard University. For coming years, Occy aspires to promote and connect people and emerging companies from his favorite cities: Palo Alto, Seattle, San Francisco, Irvine, Singapore, and Seoul.

Katie Gorick was born and raised in northern Virginia. She received a degree in Biological Engineering from the Massachusetts Institute of Technology, where she graduated with a prefect GPA (5.0 on a 5.0 scale). At MIT, Katie was a member of the Tau Beta Pi engineering honor society and a four-year varsity rower for the lightweight women's crew team. Since then, she has decided to return to her home state and pursue a PhD in Biomedical Engineering at the University of Virginia. She loves sports and outdoor activities, live music and dancing, and good food. She hopes to someday have a career designing targeted medications to more effectively treat diseases and reduce harmful side effects.

Contact Information:

Please, feel free to contact me at oscar.yang@siliconberry.com. We appreciate all kind emails.

Occy Yang

www.ingramcontent.com/pod-product-compliance
Lightning Source LLC
Chambersburg PA
CBHW071252130626
46556CB00003B/1280